PARABOLA

A NOVEL IN 21 INTERSECTIONS

by
Lily Hoang

chiasmus press
PORTLAND

CHIASMUS PRESS

www.chiasmuspress.com
press@chiasmusmedia.net

(handwritten: 2008 / 1981 / 2790.)

(handwritten: Born in 1981)

The characters and events in this book are fictitious. Any similarity to persons, living or dead, is coincidental and not intended by the author.

PRODUCED AND PRINTED IN THE UNITED STATES OF AMERICA
ISBN: 0-9815027-2-5
978-0-9815027-2-4

cover art: Bill Tourtillotte
cover design: Matthew Warren
interior design: Matthew Warren

ACKNOWLEDGEMENTS

Several chapters from this novel were first accepted elsewhere in various forms:

"Personal Equation" in *Black Warrior Review*

"News: October 11, 2005" in *Quarter After Eight*

"Period" in *From Wreckage of Reason* (anthology)

"R" in *5_Trope*

"Delta" in *Bound is the Bewitching Lilith* (anthology)

"Butterfly Effect" in *BlazeVOX*

"Home and Place" in *Square One*

A very special thanks to:
Steve Tomasula; the University of Notre Dame's MFA program, especially to my fellow workshop survivors Renée D'Aoust, Tom Miller, Dustin Rutledge, and Beth Couture; Valerie Sayers; William O'Rourke; Catherine Kasper; Lidia Yuknavitch; Trevor Dodge; Andy Mingo; Matthew Warren; both of my families; Twin Sisters; Bill Tourtillotte; and of course, Karl & our cats.

An even more special thanks to those I've somehow managed to misplace the names of in this acknowledgements page. You're the people I probably need to thank the most.

A line is a dot that went for a walk.
—PAUL KLEE

CONTENTS

ALTERNATE CONTENTS

For my family.

According to the Pythagoreans, 10 is the most perfect number. 1 is the sum of the first

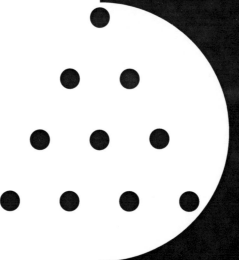

four integers, & when drawn out in dots, it makes an equilateral triangle. In this way, multiplicity becomes unity.

chapter

10

BUTTERFLY EFFECT

10

A discontented fractal causes a volcano to erupt in Sydney, Australia. The lava dances into the opera house, carrying away musicians in waves. They spill into the ocean, still playing their instruments in perfect time.

In Los Alamos, New Mexico, a physicist starts living a twenty-six hour day. He's theorized that because time is arbitrary, it wouldn't matter if a day were twenty-four or twenty-six hours long. This is his experiment, and when it fails, he wanders around the desert, half naked and mumbling how time fucked him over. He doesn't solve the mystery of time and dies a disappointment.

Anthropologists in Africa disturb the primate habitat.

He is the soloist. He can't stop just because the opera house is destroyed. He is the leader. He must lead. The cellist, playing the Dvorak Cello Concerto, the New World, pops his g-string. The strings on a cello are very thick, and he is cut across the face. His blood is the same shade of passion as the lava.

A rich man in China takes on his tenth concubine. He mail-ordered her from Vietnam. She left her country for a new life, perhaps a better life. Vietnam isn't the most luxurious place to live, but then again, neither is China. In her homeland, she lived in a hut of brown sticks glued together with the sun's heat. She constantly bled from splinters.

It was that change from twenty-four to twenty-six that catalyzed the development of chaos theory.

A twenty-year old American backpacks through Europe. He's excited. He's never traveled before. He thinks of how many other great Americans have taken this odyssey. He knows one day he'll be a great American, an American great enough for the history books. He's sure that he will bypass the simple American Dream.

Fortunately for her, he ordered her from the cheapest mail-order catalogue he could find. It didn't even have pictures. She arrives in China, a barren, paraplegic Vietnamese girl who speaks no Chinese. Their relationship is not successful. He had hoped she would bear his children, starting an entirely new race for the Chinese people.

France demands her statue back. The Divided States don't know how to react. Their princess can't be taken away like that. They will fight for her as they fight for freedom. Operation Boycott and Operation Blindfold Lady Liberty begin.

At many locations in the world, three little boys, aged four, five, and six, are molested by a teenaged boy. He shows him his cock. He asks to see theirs. He has the five-year-old suck on the four-year-old and the oldest fellates the middle boy, and he, the teenager, he does something that is unmentionable. It should remain so, but these boys will be forever damaged.

American prisons have become too full. The president decides that it would be the country's best interest to send the meddlesome inmates to Antarctica. The plans for the construction of this improved form of exile begin. Rumors leak out about the president's plan. The prisoners unite and destroy the prison facilities in over ten cities. Their effort is futile, and the president decides to punish the men by using the most cruel method of execution: death by hanging.

In Madrid, he reaches for his wallet. It was a gift from his girlfriend. He thinks about his girlfriend, how hot she is, but damn, these Spanish girls are fucking hot too. In Madrid, he reaches for his wallet that had a reptilian quality to the touch, like a tanned dragon bathing for hours in the hot jungle sun.

The monkeys ransack a small hut filled with bananas and other foods. The people are left with nothing.

When he learns that she's infertile, he orders his third mistress, his favorite, to execute the limbless whore from Vietnam. Unfortunately, women number three is near-sighted and accidentally shoots him in the groin. He will not be producing the new race for his country.

The Sydney Opera House is considered one of the seven modern wonders of the world. Its architecture creates perfect reverberations, but the lava isn't prejudiced. It swallows the opera house as it would a homeless woman's cardboard box.

A college student finds art in the form of dark matter.

A twelve-year-old in India gets his first taste of cocaine. It's bittersweet. He thinks he's getting high until his friend tells him he's sniffing baking soda. Twenty years later to the day, he is arrested for manufacturing cocaine. Twenty years later, it's the real thing.

She falls at the same moment as the eruption in Sydney.

God calls on a girl in Africa. Hallucinogenic drugs reveal his message. They're government funded drugs for HIV. They call her Mary; her name is now Mary, and she will become the New Mary and birth the second coming of the Messiah. She's not Christian, but who is she to question revelations from God? After her first fictional trimester, she vomits a million fire ants.

On the black market on an alley in St. Louis, a girl is bought. The man eats her slowly, deliberately, as he would enjoy foie gras. As their relations intensify, he has a stroke.

In Madrid, the wallet his girlfriend gave him is stolen, and without that trinket of memory, he forgets her entirely.

There are no volcanoes in Sydney.

He used to trap butterflies to watch their wings flap in struggle. The pattern on the eyes on their thin wings looked at him the way a lover would.

They swarm through the cracks of her teeth, each step burning puss.

They say that a butterfly flapping its wings in America can change the weather in China, but there is simply no way this could be true.

The Pythagoreans saw 9 as nothing more than the Magnified Sacred 3.

Of course, 3, being as magical as it was, was certainly nothing to frown upon, and being a magnified version of a most sacred number should not be an award taken lightly.

chapter

9

personal
equation

9

William Herschel, discoverer of Uranus, believed in Solarians. He didn't know that the sun was plasma, generating energy from the nuclear fusion of hydrogen into helium. Instead, William Herschel believed that the sun had a shell of phosphoric vapors, suspended

PREFACE: SOLARIANS

leagues above the surface, a continual fireworks display showcasing various shades of hot. The Solarians, he thought, were tucked beneath this fleshy layer of solar clouds, different from our clouds, something we could never really understand. The clouds on the sun blast heat, warming entire planets with light.

Texas is hot. Where he lives, the sun leaks through clothes, digging straight through skin, right to the nerve-endings. Where he lives, the Solarians have no mercy, but he doesn't know about Herschel's Solarians, peeking through their shell of cloud, staring directly down at him as he sits in his SUV. A voluntary prisoner, his body is hunched in the seat, his face sweating sour. There's only a small crack in the window, but it's a crack that's large enough for the Solarians to look at him as he uses his fingers to vacuum strands of tobacco between leather and stitching.

He's hot, trapped in his small prison. He's been a Catholic his entire life, a martyr. It must have been the martyr that told him he had to spend entire days under the

Texas sun without water. It must have been the Catholic guilt that convinced him to wash his wife's car because of a fight or some small battle waged too briefly to remember, leaving a salty resin in his mouth of her anger.

But it was neither his religion nor his wife that caused the stroke. He was too rational a man to let such trivialities wreck his body. Stuck in that car, face smashed against glass for clean air, he must have seen those Solarians, high above him, looking through their clouds into his clouds to see him, a small face against a cracked window. That must have been the reason.

Befuddled, he opens the car door, dries the car, and goes inside the house to drink a cold glass of water.

It's a well-known story for historians of science. Depending on whom you ask, it could be one of the bigger mistakes of an Astronomer Royal, a new way of yet again re-conceiving the perception of stars, the birthing of experimental psychology, or a method of measuring a person's intelligence quotient. Either way, it all relates back to 1796 and a few hundred milliseconds of skewed research.

FAIRY TALE FOR HISTORIANS OF SCIENCE

Their story is well documented, despite the fact that it was almost forgotten for nearly a quarter of a century. Of course, even that story is commonplace now.

Average reaction time and standard deviation of reaction time are correlated, but each has a unique connection with intelligence.

He notices the usual symptoms. The right side of his entire body is numb; a soft layer of distortion surrounds everyday objects. The fingers he can't quite feel look four inches thick. He says nothing. He sits this way, uncomfortable and trying to logically explain the symptoms.

He sits this way for hours until his wife comes home. In his chair, not a particularly comfortable or even special chair but a chair that he has deemed his own, he sits smoking his pipe. He hasn't unlocked the door for her as he usually does. The room is dark. He doesn't even speak to her when she walks in. So she doesn't ask. That's the nature of their relationship. Still, she knows, and she knows instantaneously.

Of course, he knows that his body has failed him. He knows that he is sweating, his body is swollen and numb, he's weaker than he's ever been, and he can't see. He knows all of this, but he refuses to accept it. He commands his body to stop it. He reasons with it that if it'll just go back to what it was, he'd be a better Catholic, he'd pray more often, he'd control his temper, he'd quit smoking, well, maybe not quit but at least cut down, he'd do anything. He isn't in pain, but his body has finally failed him. This is what he knows.

Based on the color spectrum, how would these boxes be ordered?

    A. C, B, A, D
    B. B, C, A, D
    C. D, B, C, A
    D. D, A, B, C

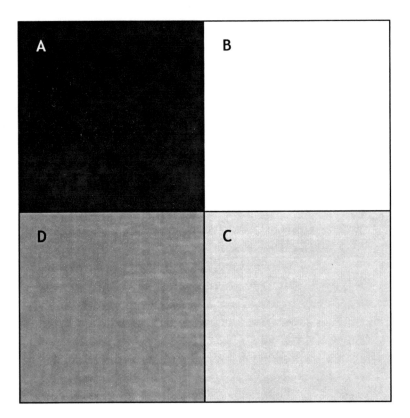

How long did it take you to answer this question?

    A. 0-5 seconds
    B. 6-15 seconds
    C. 16-30 seconds
    D. more than 31 seconds

The job, my boy, is really quite simple. Let me show you very quickly. Here now, boy, sit down and look through the telescope. What now? Well, yes of course, it is a handsome telescope, yes of course, I know. But don't distract me now, boy. Go ahead. Look through it. Well, of course it's bright! It's the afternoon! Yes, of course, I realize this. I'm not an idiot, boy! Now just listen to me for a moment, won't you? Look through the eyepiece. What do you see? Well of course you don't see anything! It's the afternoon! You're a talker, now then, aren't you? Just listen to my instructions, and listen carefully. I don't want to repeat this. At night, when you look through that same eyepiece, you'll see five vertical wires. No, boy, vertical means up and down, not across! Yes, up and down. Now just listen, won't you? The middle wire, that means the third one, corresponds with the meridian. Oh? You know what that word means, do you? I hired you to be an assistant, not to be smart with

me. Now just listen to the simple instructions. You are to be available from 7 in the morning until 10 in the evening to assist me in observations. Your job will be simple. Sit in this chair and watch objects as they pass by overhead. Now that doesn't sound so difficult, does it? Now here's the tricky part. I need you to listen to this clock. Do you hear it tick? Can you hear it clearly? Good. Now look into the telescope. When a star or any other object approaches, I want you to look at the second-hand of the clock, then note where the star is every time you hear the tick of the clock in relation to the wires. It sounds easy, doesn't it? Then all you have to do is simple mathematics to calculate the ratio of the two spatial intervals, thereby getting the moment of transit. What do you mean you don't understand? It's so simple. Where do I find imbecile assistants like you? It's quite simple. Let me explain just one more time, and my boy, you'd best listen this time.

Reaction time and standard deviation of reaction time reflect the operation of different processes.

She reasons that it's just because he hasn't eaten enough so she feeds him. She makes him his favorite meal, and he eats slowly, more slowly than he's eaten in years. He sweats. The back door is open to the diningroom table, letting in a warm breeze. They haven't turned on the air-conditioner even though this late in the evening, it's still well into the 90s; it's expensive, he reasons.

The food is bland, he says.

Let me get you some salt, she says.

Salt's bad for my body, you know that, he responds.

He gets up himself to find some seasoning. He's sweating. She sees it thick through his shirt. She is scared, not scared like she's scared of being robbed or scared of being in a car accident, even though she's scared of both those things, she's scared in a way she's never felt before. She's scared more than when the doctors told her she had cancer. She's scared more than she's scared of losing all her hair.

And, of course, he falls down.

She knew it would happen. She told him, If you don't quit smoking that pipe, something bad will happen. Sitting there, watching him fall down, she wants to scream at him, lecture him for all his stupidity. The entire family

personal equation

thinks that she's the crazy one, the one who screws up, but looking at him, she knows that she's never screwed up this big before. She watches his round body thump hard onto the tile. In her head, she's still lecturing him. Her body is confused. It doesn't know if it should get up to help him or stay put and finish dinner. He wouldn't want the help, her body tells her. Her body tells her, He's a stubborn man. Let him get up himself.

He doesn't move for a few seconds. Then, he moans, and she's sure of it.

He didn't expect this to happen. He's been running every day for half an hour. He hasn't been this healthy since he was a boy. He works outside all day, and his belly has shrunk, the same belly that his daughter used to call a watermelon; it's smaller now, like a cantaloupe. He's cut down on smoking, and still, he's on the ground. He can't understand how it all fits. He tries to make sense of it all, but the pieces are all blurry. He can't remember what he was doing or how he ended up with his face smashed against the tile. He only knows that it feels cool against the wetness of his body.

He looks up at his wife. He can only make out her shape. She's screaming, he can tell by the open blackness of her mouth, but he can't hear what she's saying. He mouths to her, Help.

She runs to the phone, dials her son's number, pauses, and hangs up. She calls an ambulance.

David Kinnebrook was only 23 when Nevil Maskelyne hired him as his personal assistant. Imagine for just one moment that you are this boy, once thought of as a precocious little boy, but precociousness doesn't last past childhood. Imagine that you have to live up to the expectations of greatness that your family arbitrarily assigned to you because they thought you were clever when you were a boy. Then, imagine that the Astronomer Royal has given *you* the opportunity to be his assistant, his one and only assistant. Of course, you're thrilled.

Life at the Greenwich Observatory isn't what you'd expect, but you didn't really know what the circumstances would be. When the Astronomer Royal speaks to you, you say, Yes sir, in response. You try to be as polite as possible. You do as you're instructed, and you try to watch the stars through the small hole and count the clicks and watch it move and count the clicks and the star has moved and you still count clicks. Then, you write down your results, employing simple mathematics. Like Dr. Maskelyne had said, it really was quite simple. You didn't expect to be counting ticks and straining already weary eyes, but still, you are proud to be his protégé.

You continue to do as you're told. You are available from 7 in the morning to late at night. You wait and watch and count. It isn't exciting or fun, but it's work, and you're the Astronomer Royal's protégé so you can't complain without feeling guilty. Still, you write home to your father from time to time to tell him how tedious work can be, how you're tired, how Dr. Maskelyne can be difficult. Your father writes back, partly trying to assuage you but mainly telling you to keep on working. Of course, you think to yourself. You have no other choices now.

One day, Dr. Maskelyne comes up to you and tells you that you've been doing things wrong. He says that there's a right way and a wrong way. Certainly, you've been doing things the wrong way. He shows you again, even though you've been doing this for a while and there isn't all that much to show that you don't already know. He says, Look at the transit wires, observe, and count.

You already know it. You try not to be insulted, but it's difficult to hold it back. You nod and assure him that it won't happen again. That day, when you observe, you are careful. You check and double-check your math. When you give him your observations, you're sure they're accurate. He doesn't say anything the next day so you think that you're safe. You continue to be careful. Every observation is precious to you. You are proud of yourself. You are proud of your work.

What is the missing letter?

A. I
B. W
C. M
D. C

B	A	C
C	B	E
E	C	H
H	E	?

The more complex the reaction time task, the greater the influence of intraindividual variability.

By the time the ambulance arrives, she's called her son and oldest daughter. Her son has a habit of ignoring her calls so when he sees her number flashing on his cell phone, he doesn't pick up. Like a good Catholic boy, he feels guilty while checking voicemail. Her voice shakes through his ears. John, it says, this is your mom. Your dad, he. And that's where he stops it. He calls his mother, still feeling guilty, and dashes to their aid. He's always wanted to be their Prince Charming, but he perpetually fails expectations.

The moment she tells him the symptoms, he tells her that it wasn't a heart attack, that she should calm down because he'll be all right. He lies to her. From what she told him, he knows that his father didn't have a heart attack. He knows that he had a stroke. He knows because he should have been a doctor. He could have been a doctor. But he dropped out. He never tells his family the reason why he simply quit right before he finished his dissertation and a year before completing medical school. He'd been in school for over a decade. He did all of it for his parents to be happy, to be proud, but he couldn't sustain it. He ignores his mother's calls because she makes him feel guilty about school, but when her voice is flustered, he forgives both of them. He wouldn't want to admit it, but he's scared for his father.

Scared and nervous, speeding down I-35, he calls his baby sister. She doesn't have a cell phone, so he calls her boyfriend's. No one picks up. He knows that her boyfriend's family doesn't like to pick up the phone. He calls again. And again. He calls over fifteen time before reaching the hospital.

Nervous energy trips him out of the car, and he falls down. His mother rushes out of the emergency room to kiss his pain away.

Martha, she says, your dad just fell down.

What d'you mean, fell down?

I think he had a heart attack, but John said that it wasn't, but he said he doesn't know what happened. He thinks maybe he was just dehydrated, but he was sweating. He was sweating a lot, and he said he couldn't taste his food, and then he got up to get something, and he just fell down. Just like that, and he was down on the ground.

Mommy, listen to me. It's going to be ok. Do you want me to come home? Do I need to be there?

Oh Martha. I'm so scared. What if he dies? I have nothing. I have no one.

Calm down, mother! It'll be ok. Do you want me to come home? I can get a plane down there tomorrow morning.

Your father might die.

Martha is two states away from her family. She has a son and a husband that she can't leave. Even as she offers to come home, she knows that she can't. She doesn't believe her mother that her father is in such a dire state. She tries to ignore it. Her family is hard on her. She's the oldest. She was supposed to be the first one to achieve the American dream, but she didn't. Instead, she ran away from home and rebelled any way she could. She tries to ignore this version of her past by telling people that she went to college in Louisiana and majored in architecture. Her husband believes this. So does her son. She even believes it, but her family doesn't. They know all the small truths she's stowed away. She tries to displace those enemies, but they're family.

In her mother's voice, she recognizes the immediacy of the situation, but she can't translate it into something that she knows. She can't understand what just happened.

The rest of the story is part of the fabric of historical mythology. Maskelyne continues to find errors in Kinnebrook's work, and he eventually fires him in the winter of 1796. The largest discrepancy between the Astronomer Royal's observation and his assistant's was 800 milliseconds. Maskelyne believed there should be no more than a 100 msec margin of error.

In 1821, Friedrich Bessel reviewed all of the logs from that time. From this, he derived that both of their observations were correct. He asserted that every person has a different reaction time to sensory stimulus, which accounted for Kinnebrook's consistent transit times and how they were different from Maskelyne's measurements.

It is rare that an assistant is cleared from shame in this way, but that is what makes this story so special. That, and of course, all of the other details that historians have forgotten to include.

Which comes next in the sequence?

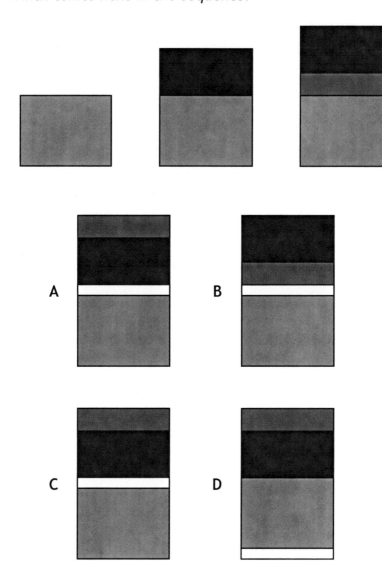

How long did it take you to answer this question?
- **A.** 0-5 seconds
- **B.** 6-15 seconds
- **C.** 16-30 seconds
- **D.** more than 31 seconds

The contribution of intraindividual variability increases as the Intelligence Quotient (IQ) decreases.

She walks into his house after dinner. They went to have steak, and she doesn't eat meat. She had potatoes cooked four different ways, each one equally unpalatable. His mom says, I think you got some phone calls. It looks like John called you a bunch of times.

She knows it instantly. Before even picking up the telephone to call him, she lights a cigarette and falls onto the sofa. When his voice tells her, she doesn't speak. She doesn't say anything until she's in the car, driving to the hospital, and when she does speak, her whispers are barely audible.

When she arrives at the hospital, she is the last one in the family to arrive, except Martha, who can't come because she's still in Colorado. Even all of her extended family is there. When she arrives at the hospital, her father is awake. She runs to him and tightly grabs his right hand. He says, I love you, but I can't feel your hand. Please, squeeze it tighter so I can feel it.

THE FALL (II)

In 1794, Neville Maskelyne hired a young boy of 23 to be his assistant. The boy's name was David Kinnebrook. The assistant was bright and quite cheerful […]

[…] but he was a dreadful klutz. People at the observatory even named him Kinnebroken. He thought it was endearing until he broke the plumb line of the south mural quadrant in particularly cold January 1795. His nickname became prophecy. Within the following year and a half, Kinnebrook broke at least four perpendicular wires of the transit instrument.

Before he could break anything else, Maskelyne approached him to discuss his position at the observatory. He said, Dave, my boy, let me start by saying that I think you're a fine lad, but you lack the necessary traits to be a good astronomer. I've repeatedly tried to help you with

your flawed observational techniques, but I fear that yours is a case that is simply impossible. I'm sorry, but I must replace you with some one more suitable for this demanding position.

Kinnebrook responded, But sir, I've not done anything wrong.

Unaccustomed to this sort of conflict, Maskelyne bitingly spit out, Your judgments of transit times were quite often more than 800 msecs off, and for that, you are dismissed!

[…] and Dr. Maskelyne was more than fond of him. It wasn't long after Kinnebrook arrived that the Astronomer Royal invited him to join his family for dinner. When the assistant politely declined, he was more strongly urged until he was no longer given an option. This continued to be the extant of their relationship, that of offerer and decliner; however, Dr. Maskelyne's offers were never mere offers. As soon as Kinnebrook declined, as he inevitably did with every invitation, he was given second and third opportunities to answer correctly. The assistant became a mouse trained by shock and stimulus. He quickly learned that he could not, under any circumstance, say no to his employer.

Once, however, he was overwhelmed with work. He insisted that he couldn't go to dinner. He complained that his workload was too great and that he had no other option but to skip dinner entirely. He even went so far as to say that dinner with the Maskelynes could be as tedious as transit time.

Before he could say anything else, Maskelyne approached him to discuss his position at the observatory. He said, Dave, my boy, let me start by saying that I think you're a fine lad, but you lack the necessary traits to be a good astronomer. I've repeatedly tried to help you with your flawed observational techniques, but I fear that yours is a case that is simply impossible. I'm sorry, but I must replace you with some one more suitable for this demanding position.

Kinnebrook responded, But sir, I've not done anything wrong.

Unaccustomed to this sort of conflict, Maskelyne bitingly spit out, Your judgments of transit times were quite often more than 800 msecs off, and for that, you are dismissed!

[…] and undeniably good-looking. Dr. Maskelyne's friend had a daughter whom was recently widowed. She was a beautiful woman, although a bit older than Kinnebrook.

The Astronomer Royal was fond of his assistant and wanted him to marry into both wealth and respect, and he gave his assistant a firm blessing for the hypothetical union.

Soon, Kinnebrook was invited to dinner every evening with this woman and the Maskelynes, and despite his mounting pile of work, he was obliged to their company. Although he was compelled to spend evenings with them, he secretly wrote to his father and begged for advice. When his father told him that it was not his duty to the Greenwich Observatory to marry this woman, he promptly spoke to his employer.

Before he could assert his displeasure, Maskelyne approached him to discuss his position at the observatory. He said, Dave, my boy, let me start by saying that I think you're a fine lad, but you lack the necessary traits to be a good astronomer. I've repeatedly tried to help you with your flawed observational techniques, but I fear that yours is a case that is simply impossible. I'm sorry, but I must replace you with some one more suitable for this demanding position.

Kinnebrook responded, But sir, I've not done anything wrong.

Unaccustomed to this sort of conflict, Maskelyne bitingly spit out, Your judgments of transit times were quite often more than 800 msecs off, and for that, you are dismissed!

[...] and quite secretive. Against Maskelyne's wishes, Kinnebrook began corresponding with William Herschel about some comets. Herschel never criticized him for transit time errors, nor did he force meals on him. Kinnebrook enjoyed Dr. Herschel's kindness, more like a fatherly nurturing than a frustrated smothering.

One day, Dr. Maskelyne found the letters. Before Kinnebrook could explain, Maskelyne approached him to discuss his position at the observatory. He said, Dave, my boy, let me start by saying that I think you're a fine lad, but you lack the necessary traits to be a good astronomer. I've repeatedly tried to help you with your flawed observational techniques, but I fear that yours is a case that is simply impossible. I'm sorry, but I must replace you with some one more suitable for this demanding position.

Kinnebrook responded, But sir, I've not done anything wrong.

Unaccustomed to this sort of conflict, Maskelyne bitingly spit out, Your judgments of transit times were quite often more than 800 msecs off, and for that, you are dismissed!

[...] but he was simply a terrible astronomer. He couldn't understand how to measure transit time. One day, Maskelyne approached him to discuss his position at the observatory. He said, Dave, my boy, let me start by saying that I think you're a fine lad, but you lack the necessary traits to be a good astronomer. I've repeatedly tried to help you with your flawed observational techniques, but I fear that yours is a case that is simply impossible. I'm sorry, but I must replace you with some one more suitable for this demanding position.

Kinnebrook responded, But sir, I've not done anything wrong.

Unaccustomed to this sort of conflict, Maskelyne bitingly spit out, Your judgments of transit times were quite often more than 800 msecs off, and for that, you are dismissed!

Which of the following words can be spelled using only the letters in "ambidextrous"?

    A. score

    B. spade

    C. braid

    D.

How long did it take you to answer this question?

    A. 0-5 seconds

    B. 6-15 seconds

    C. 16-30 seconds

    D. more than 31 seconds

There are strong neurological and genetic influences on intraindividual variability.

The characters in this story have had their Intelligence Quotient measured by traditional methods of intelligence testing. This is how the family ranks:

1. Father
2. Son
3. Youngest daughter
4. Mother
5. Oldest daughter

RISING AND FALLING

The oldest daughter started a multimillion dollar construction company without a high school diploma.

The mother has always been thought of as absent-minded. She makes poor business decisions and once asked her daughter whether there were sixty pennies in a dollar or sixty minutes in an hour.

The son remains a dissertation away from a Ph.D. in neuropharmacology and a year from an M.D. He is a waiter.

The father was once a mathematics professor, but a war tore him from his native tongue. He was a maintenance man for the state hospital for twenty-five years before retiring.

The youngest daughter gardens and does yoga daily. She has no claimed profession.

This is the ranking of quickness in reaction time measured from the point that the stroke occurred to the moment of realization:

1. Mother
2. Son
3. Oldest Daughter
4. Youngest Daughter
5. Father

This variability in reaction time has been called Personal Equation. Most psychologists believe that there is a correlation between intelligence and personal equation.

He still goes outside to work in his garden. Even though the left side of his body is bloated numb, he insists upon spending at least an hour working outside every day. Perhaps he is still looking for the Solarians.

POST-SCRIPT: THE SOLARIANS (III)

Ancient Greek mathematicians, including the Pythagorean, believed that 8 was the most lucky number. There is little explanation of why they believed this.

These mathematicians also found that every odd number greater than 1, when squared,

results in a multiple of 8 plus 1. For instance, $5^2 = 25 = (3 \times 8) + 1$.

Also, every odd number greater than 1, when squared, will differ the previous odd number squared by a multiple of 8. For instance, $9^2 - 7^2 = 81 - 62 = 32 =$ x 8.

chapter

8

: personality
indicator
(version 8.0)

8

INSTRUCTIONS: Please answer the following questions in the most honest manner possible. This test is constructed to force decisions. In order to reduce the margin of error, there is only a small degree of middle ground, thereby forcing you to use gut instinct. Please remember that this is a timed test. You will have twenty minutes to complete this survey. Any questions left unanswered will be scored against you. Thank you and please do enjoy.

1. I take on many tasks at the same time.
EXTREMELY INACCURATE   ①   ②   ③   ④   EXTREMELY ACCURATE

2. I like to read directions.
EXTREMELY INACCURATE   ①   ②   ③   ④   EXTREMELY ACCURATE

3. I find pain strangely satisfying.
EXTREMELY INACCURATE   ①   ②   ③   ④   EXTREMELY ACCURATE

4. Money is the most important thing to me.
EXTREMELY INACCURATE   ①   ②   ③   ④   EXTREMELY ACCURATE

5. I don't mind blowing people off.
EXTREMELY INACCURATE   ①   ②   ③   ④   EXTREMELY ACCURATE

6. I don't believe in hierarchies.
EXTREMELY INACCURATE   ①   ②   ③   ④   EXTREMELY ACCURATE

7. I reward myself with intellectual pain.
EXTREMELY INACCURATE   ①   ②   ③   ④   EXTREMELY ACCURATE

8. I use logic to make decisions.
EXTREMELY INACCURATE   ①   ②   ③   ④   EXTREMELY ACCURATE

9. I find activities boring unless I play the dominant role.
EXTREMELY INACCURATE   ①   ②   ③   ④   EXTREMELY ACCURATE

10. I'm not very active.

EXTREMELY INACCURATE   ①   ②   ③   ④   EXTREMELY ACCURATE

11. I have a strong personality.

EXTREMELY INACCURATE   ①   ②   ③   ④   EXTREMELY ACCURATE

12. I like to think.

EXTREMELY INACCURATE   ①   ②   ③   ④   EXTREMELY ACCURATE

13. I'm practically suicidal.

EXTREMELY INACCURATE   ①   ②   ③   ④   EXTREMELY ACCURATE

14. I love to travel and see new sites.

EXTREMELY INACCURATE   ①   ②   ③   ④   EXTREMELY ACCURATE

15. I finish what I start.

EXTREMELY INACCURATE   ①   ②   ③   ④   EXTREMELY ACCURATE

16. I am determined.

EXTREMELY INACCURATE   ①   ②   ③   ④   EXTREMELY ACCURATE

17. I am more passive than active.

EXTREMELY INACCURATE   ①   ②   ③   ④   EXTREMELY ACCURATE

18. I put the need of others before my own.

EXTREMELY INACCURATE   ①   ②   ③   ④   EXTREMELY ACCURATE

19. I have seen my parents have sexual intercourse.

EXTREMELY INACCURATE   ①   ②   ③   ④   EXTREMELY ACCURATE

20. Many people think I am cold and uncaring.

EXTREMELY INACCURATE   ①   ②   ③   ④   EXTREMELY ACCURATE

21. I want to be rich.

EXTREMELY INACCURATE   ①   ②   ③   ④   EXTREMELY ACCURATE

22. I prefer to live in my own head sometimes.

EXTREMELY INACCURATE   ①   ②   ③   ④   EXTREMELY ACCURATE

23. I have faith in humanity.

EXTREMELY INACCURATE   ①   ②   ③   ④   EXTREMELY ACCURATE

24. When I'm bored, I will read an instruction manual.

EXTREMELY INACCURATE   ①   ②   ③   ④   EXTREMELY ACCURATE

25. I have had sexual relations with someone in my family.

EXTREMELY INACCURATE   ①   ②   ③   ④   EXTREMELY ACCURATE

26. I keep myself busy.

EXTREMELY INACCURATE   ①   ②   ③   ④   EXTREMELY ACCURATE

27. I am passionate.

EXTREMELY INACCURATE   ①   ②   ③   ④   EXTREMELY ACCURATE

28. I love meeting new people.

EXTREMELY INACCURATE   ①   ②   ③   ④   EXTREMELY ACCURATE

29. I am egotistical.

EXTREMELY INACCURATE   ①   ②   ③   ④   EXTREMELY ACCURATE

30. I masturbate.

EXTREMELY INACCURATE   ①   ②   ③   ④   EXTREMELY ACCURATE

31. I'm ashamed that I masturbate.

EXTREMELY INACCURATE   ①   ②   ③   ④   EXTREMELY ACCURATE

32. I am reactionary.

EXTREMELY INACCURATE   ①   ②   ③   ④   EXTREMELY ACCURATE

33. I donate old things rather than throw them away.

EXTREMELY INACCURATE   ①   ②   ③   ④   EXTREMELY ACCURATE

34. I spend a lot of time thinking.

EXTREMELY INACCURATE   ①   ②   ③   ④   EXTREMELY ACCURATE

35. Appearances matter to me.

EXTREMELY INACCURATE   ①   ②   ③   ④   EXTREMELY ACCURATE

36. People below me on the social hierarchy aren't important.
EXTREMELY INACCURATE   ①   ②   ③   ④   EXTREMELY ACCURATE

37. I am a vegetarian.
EXTREMELY INACCURATE   ①   ②   ③   ④   EXTREMELY ACCURATE

38. I like to exercise to look good.
EXTREMELY INACCURATE   ①   ②   ③   ④   EXTREMELY ACCURATE

39. I am very rational.
EXTREMELY INACCURATE   ①   ②   ③   ④   EXTREMELY ACCURATE

40. I feel bad if I hurt someone's feelings.
EXTREMELY INACCURATE   ①   ②   ③   ④   EXTREMELY ACCURATE

41. I have a lot of pent up anger.
EXTREMELY INACCURATE   ①   ②   ③   ④   EXTREMELY ACCURATE

42. I am aggressive.
EXTREMELY INACCURATE   ①   ②   ③   ④   EXTREMELY ACCURATE

43. I am always trying to improve myself.
EXTREMELY INACCURATE   ①   ②   ③   ④   EXTREMELY ACCURATE

44. I have agoraphobia.
EXTREMELY INACCURATE   ①   ②   ③   ④   EXTREMELY ACCURATE

45. Some people think I'm lazy.
EXTREMELY INACCURATE   ①   ②   ③   ④   EXTREMELY ACCURATE

46. I am spontaneous.
EXTREMELY INACCURATE   ①   ②   ③   ④   EXTREMELY ACCURATE

47. In relationships, I am always the dominant one.
EXTREMELY INACCURATE   ①   ②   ③   ④   EXTREMELY ACCURATE

48. I am provocative.
EXTREMELY INACCURATE   ①   ②   ③   ④   EXTREMELY ACCURATE

49. I like to follow instructions.

EXTREMELY INACCURATE   ①   ②   ③   ④   EXTREMELY ACCURATE

50. People take advantage of me.

EXTREMELY INACCURATE   ①   ②   ③   ④   EXTREMELY ACCURATE

51. My close friends are afraid I will physically hurt them.

EXTREMELY INACCURATE   ①   ②   ③   ④   EXTREMELY ACCURATE

52. People's opinions matter to me.

EXTREMELY INACCURATE   ①   ②   ③   ④   EXTREMELY ACCURATE

53. I am comfortable with the unknown.

EXTREMELY INACCURATE   ①   ②   ③   ④   EXTREMELY ACCURATE

54. I have connections.

EXTREMELY INACCURATE   ①   ②   ③   ④   EXTREMELY ACCURATE

55. I like to work with my hands.

EXTREMELY INACCURATE   ①   ②   ③   ④   EXTREMELY ACCURATE

56. I believe in conspiracy theories.

EXTREMELY INACCURATE   ①   ②   ③   ④   EXTREMELY ACCURATE

57. I like to push those around me to be better.

EXTREMELY INACCURATE   ①   ②   ③   ④   EXTREMELY ACCURATE

58. I take my time in life.

EXTREMELY INACCURATE   ①   ②   ③   ④   EXTREMELY ACCURATE

59. New people excite me.

EXTREMELY INACCURATE   ①   ②   ③   ④   EXTREMELY ACCURATE

60. I value time by myself.

EXTREMELY INACCURATE   ①   ②   ③   ④   EXTREMELY ACCURATE

61. Sometimes, people think I'm pushy.

EXTREMELY INACCURATE   ①   ②   ③   ④   EXTREMELY ACCURATE

62. I complete tasks with care.
EXTREMELY INACCURATE ① ② ③ ④ EXTREMELY ACCURATE

63. My sexual partners are weak and submissive.
EXTREMELY INACCURATE ① ② ③ ④ EXTREMELY ACCURATE

64. I think about the future.
EXTREMELY INACCURATE ① ② ③ ④ EXTREMELY ACCURATE

65. I am sexually excited by numbers and/or science.
EXTREMELY INACCURATE ① ② ③ ④ EXTREMELY ACCURATE

66. I tip below 15%, unless I get really exceptional service.
EXTREMELY INACCURATE ① ② ③ ④ EXTREMELY ACCURATE

67. I don't need fame.
EXTREMELY INACCURATE ① ② ③ ④ EXTREMELY ACCURATE

68. I enjoy studying maps.
EXTREMELY INACCURATE ① ② ③ ④ EXTREMELY ACCURATE

69. I enjoy inflicting pain on others.
EXTREMELY INACCURATE ① ② ③ ④ EXTREMELY ACCURATE

70. No one matters but me. I'm the most important.
EXTREMELY INACCURATE ① ② ③ ④ EXTREMELY ACCURATE

71. I am a natural leader.
EXTREMELY INACCURATE ① ② ③ ④ EXTREMELY ACCURATE

72. I de-construct things.
EXTREMELY INACCURATE ① ② ③ ④ EXTREMELY ACCURATE

73. I care about your pain.
EXTREMELY INACCURATE ① ② ③ ④ EXTREMELY ACCURATE

74. I am always prepared.
EXTREMELY INACCURATE ① ② ③ ④ EXTREMELY ACCURATE

75. I love star-gazing.

EXTREMELY INACCURATE   ①   ②   ③   ④   EXTREMELY ACCURATE

76. I play through scenes with various courses of action before acting.

EXTREMELY INACCURATE   ①   ②   ③   ④   EXTREMELY ACCURATE

77. I am very popular.

EXTREMELY INACCURATE   ①   ②   ③   ④   EXTREMELY ACCURATE

78. I will be rich and famous one day.

EXTREMELY INACCURATE   ①   ②   ③   ④   EXTREMELY ACCURATE

79. I am the boss.

EXTREMELY INACCURATE   ①   ②   ③   ④   EXTREMELY ACCURATE

80. I'm not afraid to ask for directions.

EXTREMELY INACCURATE   ①   ②   ③   ④   EXTREMELY ACCURATE

81. I prefer wide, open spaces to city life.

EXTREMELY INACCURATE   ①   ②   ③   ④   EXTREMELY ACCURATE

82. I can spend hours at a museum.

EXTREMELY INACCURATE   ①   ②   ③   ④   EXTREMELY ACCURATE

83. I am exactly who I want to be.

EXTREMELY INACCURATE   ①   ②   ③   ④   EXTREMELY ACCURATE

84. I like long walks on the beach and watching sunsets.

EXTREMELY INACCURATE   ①   ②   ③   ④   EXTREMELY ACCURATE

85. I care about what people think about me.

EXTREMELY INACCURATE   ①   ②   ③   ④   EXTREMELY ACCURATE

86. I don't like debating.

EXTREMELY INACCURATE   ①   ②   ③   ④   EXTREMELY ACCURATE

87. It's ok to start at the bottom and work your way to the top, as long as you get there.

EXTREMELY INACCURATE   ①   ②   ③   ④   EXTREMELY ACCURATE

88.   I always feel rushed.

EXTREMELY INACCURATE   ①   ②   ③   ④   EXTREMELY ACCURATE

89.   I feel rushed right now.

EXTREMELY INACCURATE   ①   ②   ③   ④   EXTREMELY ACCURATE

90.   Some people think I'm weak.

EXTREMELY INACCURATE   ①   ②   ③   ④   EXTREMELY ACCURATE

91.   I multitask.

EXTREMELY INACCURATE   ①   ②   ③   ④   EXTREMELY ACCURATE

92.   I can spend hours thinking.

EXTREMELY INACCURATE   ①   ②   ③   ④   EXTREMELY ACCURATE

93.   The few close friends I have are very important to me.

EXTREMELY INACCURATE   ①   ②   ③   ④   EXTREMELY ACCURATE

94.   I analyze things objectively and critically.

EXTREMELY INACCURATE   ①   ②   ③   ④   EXTREMELY ACCURATE

95.   I dress well.

EXTREMELY INACCURATE   ①   ②   ③   ④   EXTREMELY ACCURATE

96.   I take things apart and put them back together.

EXTREMELY INACCURATE   ①   ②   ③   ④   EXTREMELY ACCURATE

97.   I bleed often.

EXTREMELY INACCURATE   ①   ②   ③   ④   EXTREMELY ACCURATE

98.   I believe in hierarchies.

EXTREMELY INACCURATE   ①   ②   ③   ④   EXTREMELY ACCURATE

99.   I put the needs of others before my own,
        even if could be hurt by it.

EXTREMELY INACCURATE   ①   ②   ③   ④   EXTREMELY ACCURATE

100.   I am not aggressive.

EXTREMELY INACCURATE   ①   ②   ③   ④   EXTREMELY ACCURATE

101. I have a strong personality.
EXTREMELY INACCURATE ① ② ③ ④ EXTREMELY ACCURATE

102. I am not provocative.
EXTREMELY INACCURATE ① ② ③ ④ EXTREMELY ACCURATE

103. People are important to me.
EXTREMELY INACCURATE ① ② ③ ④ EXTREMELY ACCURATE

104. I am always the center of attention.
EXTREMELY INACCURATE ① ② ③ ④ EXTREMELY ACCURATE

105. I always think before acting.
EXTREMELY INACCURATE ① ② ③ ④ EXTREMELY ACCURATE

106. I think highly of myself.
EXTREMELY INACCURATE ① ② ③ ④ EXTREMELY ACCURATE

107. I'm messy.
EXTREMELY INACCURATE ① ② ③ ④ EXTREMELY ACCURATE

108. I would volunteer my services to anyone who needed it.
EXTREMELY INACCURATE ① ② ③ ④ EXTREMELY ACCURATE

109. One day, I will have a building named after me.
EXTREMELY INACCURATE ① ② ③ ④ EXTREMELY ACCURATE

110. I prefer to look at the pieces that make up bigger things.
EXTREMELY INACCURATE ① ② ③ ④ EXTREMELY ACCURATE

111. I don't have many close friends.
EXTREMELY INACCURATE ① ② ③ ④ EXTREMELY ACCURATE

112. I'm pretty sure I'm a rational person.
EXTREMELY INACCURATE ① ② ③ ④ EXTREMELY ACCURATE

113. I often find myself in compromising situations.
EXTREMELY INACCURATE ① ② ③ ④ EXTREMELY ACCURATE

114. Multiple choice tests are useless.
EXTREMELY INACCURATE ① ② ③ ④ EXTREMELY ACCURATE

115. I like to plan things.
EXTREMELY INACCURATE ① ② ③ ④ EXTREMELY ACCURATE

116. I'm a perfectionist.
EXTREMELY INACCURATE ① ② ③ ④ EXTREMELY ACCURATE

117. I don't like to fight.
EXTREMELY INACCURATE ① ② ③ ④ EXTREMELY ACCURATE

118. Other people sway my decision-making.
EXTREMELY INACCURATE ① ② ③ ④ EXTREMELY ACCURATE

119. My parents worry that I hurt myself.
EXTREMELY INACCURATE ① ② ③ ④ EXTREMELY ACCURATE

120. I sometimes forget that other people are around me.
EXTREMELY INACCURATE ① ② ③ ④ EXTREMELY ACCURATE

121. Many people acknowledge that I am good-looking.
EXTREMELY INACCURATE ① ② ③ ④ EXTREMELY ACCURATE

122. I act before thinking.
EXTREMELY INACCURATE ① ② ③ ④ EXTREMELY ACCURATE

123. People are amazed by what I produce.
EXTREMELY INACCURATE ① ② ③ ④ EXTREMELY ACCURATE

124. I have a very active social life.
EXTREMELY INACCURATE ① ② ③ ④ EXTREMELY ACCURATE

125. Some people find me overbearing.
EXTREMELY INACCURATE ① ② ③ ④ EXTREMELY ACCURATE

126. I would hurt anyone if it would help me.
EXTREMELY INACCURATE ① ② ③ ④ EXTREMELY ACCURATE

127. I make people feel loved.
EXTREMELY INACCURATE ① ② ③ ④ EXTREMELY ACCURATE

128. I only eat organic food.
EXTREMELY INACCURATE ① ② ③ ④ EXTREMELY ACCURATE

129. I'm not very popular.
EXTREMELY INACCURATE ① ② ③ ④ EXTREMELY ACCURATE

130. It's definitely not ok to leave a task incomplete.
EXTREMELY INACCURATE ① ② ③ ④ EXTREMELY ACCURATE

131. I like to think over problems until I find the perfect solution.
EXTREMELY INACCURATE ① ② ③ ④ EXTREMELY ACCURATE

132. Sometimes, I let people take of advantage of me.
EXTREMELY INACCURATE ① ② ③ ④ EXTREMELY ACCURATE

133. I am not a planner.
EXTREMELY INACCURATE ① ② ③ ④ EXTREMELY ACCURATE

134. I have a very high IQ.
EXTREMELY INACCURATE ① ② ③ ④ EXTREMELY ACCURATE

135. People think I am very strong.
EXTREMELY INACCURATE ① ② ③ ④ EXTREMELY ACCURATE

136. I take my time.
EXTREMELY INACCURATE ① ② ③ ④ EXTREMELY ACCURATE

137. Equality doesn't exist. It never will, and people who think that it will are naïve fools.
EXTREMELY INACCURATE ① ② ③ ④ EXTREMELY ACCURATE

138. I am esoteric.
EXTREMELY INACCURATE ① ② ③ ④ EXTREMELY ACCURATE

139. I spend a lot of time thinking before I act.
EXTREMELY INACCURATE ① ② ③ ④ EXTREMELY ACCURATE

140. My feelings are hurt when someone argues with me.
EXTREMELY INACCURATE   ①   ②   ③   ④   EXTREMELY ACCURATE

141. Even I think I'm egotistical.
EXTREMELY INACCURATE   ①   ②   ③   ④   EXTREMELY ACCURATE

142. The means are more important than the end.
EXTREMELY INACCURATE   ①   ②   ③   ④   EXTREMELY ACCURATE

143. Meeting new people scares me.
EXTREMELY INACCURATE   ①   ②   ③   ④   EXTREMELY ACCURATE

144. I like to fight with people.
EXTREMELY INACCURATE   ①   ②   ③   ④   EXTREMELY ACCURATE

145. I want to hurt anybody.
EXTREMELY INACCURATE   ①   ②   ③   ④   EXTREMELY ACCURATE

146. I'm highly motivated.
EXTREMELY INACCURATE   ①   ②   ③   ④   EXTREMELY ACCURATE

147. I like to look at beautiful things.
EXTREMELY INACCURATE   ①   ②   ③   ④   EXTREMELY ACCURATE

148. I would rather fix something than replace it.
EXTREMELY INACCURATE   ①   ②   ③   ④   EXTREMELY ACCURATE

149. I've punched someone unconscious.
EXTREMELY INACCURATE   ①   ②   ③   ④   EXTREMELY ACCURATE

150. I don't plan my life.
EXTREMELY INACCURATE   ①   ②   ③   ④   EXTREMELY ACCURATE

151. I am completely focused on whatever I'm working on.
EXTREMELY INACCURATE   ①   ②   ③   ④   EXTREMELY ACCURATE

152. I grind my teeth at night.
EXTREMELY INACCURATE   ①   ②   ③   ④   EXTREMELY ACCURATE

153. I'm sometimes accused of not living in this world.
EXTREMELY INACCURATE   ①   ②   ③   ④   EXTREMELY ACCURATE

154. I'm egocentric.
EXTREMELY INACCURATE   ①   ②   ③   ④   EXTREMELY ACCURATE

155. Emotions get in the way.
EXTREMELY INACCURATE   ①   ②   ③   ④   EXTREMELY ACCURATE

156. I am always growing and changing.
EXTREMELY INACCURATE   ①   ②   ③   ④   EXTREMELY ACCURATE

157. I'm a loner.
EXTREMELY INACCURATE   ①   ②   ③   ④   EXTREMELY ACCURATE

158. I read books.
EXTREMELY INACCURATE   ①   ②   ③   ④   EXTREMELY ACCURATE

159. I am provocative.
EXTREMELY INACCURATE   ①   ②   ③   ④   EXTREMELY ACCURATE

160. I am rational.
EXTREMELY INACCURATE   ①   ②   ③   ④   EXTREMELY ACCURATE

161. The world is beautiful.
EXTREMELY INACCURATE   ①   ②   ③   ④   EXTREMELY ACCURATE

162. People are morons.
EXTREMELY INACCURATE   ①   ②   ③   ④   EXTREMELY ACCURATE

163. I'm brilliant.
EXTREMELY INACCURATE   ①   ②   ③   ④   EXTREMELY ACCURATE

164. I've never had an orgasm.
EXTREMELY INACCURATE   ①   ②   ③   ④   EXTREMELY ACCURATE

165. Consequences don't exist for me.
EXTREMELY INACCURATE   ①   ②   ③   ④   EXTREMELY ACCURATE

166. Salt is bad for the body.

EXTREMELY INACCURATE   ①   ②   ③   ④   EXTREMELY ACCURATE

167. I'm co-dependent.

EXTREMELY INACCURATE   ①   ②   ③   ④   EXTREMELY ACCURATE

168. Money doesn't drive me.

EXTREMELY INACCURATE   ①   ②   ③   ④   EXTREMELY ACCURATE

169. It takes time to get ready.

EXTREMELY INACCURATE   ①   ②   ③   ④   EXTREMELY ACCURATE

170. I'm indie.

EXTREMELY INACCURATE   ①   ②   ③   ④   EXTREMELY ACCURATE

171. My iPod matches my Mac.

EXTREMELY INACCURATE   ①   ②   ③   ④   EXTREMELY ACCURATE

172. Saving the world is a realistic goal.

EXTREMELY INACCURATE   ①   ②   ③   ④   EXTREMELY ACCURATE

173. I've got a real job.

EXTREMELY INACCURATE   ①   ②   ③   ④   EXTREMELY ACCURATE

174. I provoke arguments.

EXTREMELY INACCURATE   ①   ②   ③   ④   EXTREMELY ACCURATE

175. I am artistic.

EXTREMELY INACCURATE   ①   ②   ③   ④   EXTREMELY ACCURATE

Thank you for completing the *Personality Indicator.*

Please give us one moment to tabulate your score. While we do so, please read about the various personality types. You will be neatly categorized very shortly. Thank you for your patience.

PERSONALITY TYPES

DOERS: rarely have time for fun. They're always doing something, and that something is generally useful. That's not to say that they never have fun, but for a Doer, fun has a designated time and space, and if life throws this fun time a lemon, the Doer doesn't make lemonade; he makes lemongrass. Doers are particularly special people because they do more than expected and exceed everyone's expectations. Generally, Doers don't have any friends, partially because no one can stand an ass kisser and partially because Doers can't take enough time out of their immaculately planned days to make or maintain friends. It's a lonely life.

THINKERS: never shut up. Unlike the Doer though, he never actually gets anything done. All that the Thinker does is talk and talk about whatever it is that he's trying to figure out. Often, Thinkers develop some sort of sleeping dysfunction, whether it's sleep talking or violent behavior during the REM stage. These are common warning signs for schizophrenia, which many Thinkers are afflicted with. Thinkers tend to develop this illness because their thoughts are in constant competition with each other, and the Thinker himself is left dumbstruck as to which voice or argument to believe. In general, Thinkers don't live past the age of twenty-six and a half. The most common method of suicide is death by hanging.

ACTIVE: personalities tend to be strong characters. They exude a sense of determination & can be seen as aggressive. An Active personality often resorts to alcohol to calm himself down after such an Active day. He's exhausted and irritable, which is why the slightest provocation can bring about a frenzied rage. During these rages, the Active personality dominates all other personality traits, and the person blocks out all memory of this time. It is not uncommon for unusually violent behavior, mostly rape and other sexual molestations, to be exhibited during this time. They are only trying to actively engage whatever it is that they are currently focusing on. Active personalities tend to try to blaze through tasks. Active personalities have a better understanding of self because they are always trying to improve themselves. They tend to be provocateurs.

REACTIVE: personalities do not act until provoked. They will tend to be the followers and follow directions perfectly. They do not deal well with authority, unless there is someone above them giving them instructions. It is not that Reactive personalities are submissive. It is just that they prefer to react to situations rather than provoke them. Reactive personalities also tend to carefully complete tasks. Reactive personalities make excellent stalkers and assassins because they covet any assignment as though it was made of solid bronze.

SADIST: personalities tend to let emotion dictate action. This is not to say that whatever decision is made will be the most "caring" though. Rather, Sadist personality only means that they prefer to consider the repercussions of their actions on those around them before acting. Because sadism has been given a negative connotation in today's society, it is important for one to understand the positive aspects of the Sadist personality. Sadists tend to be most kind and caring people, much more so than any other personality type.

MASOCHIST: personalities tend to let rational thought dictate action. This is not to say that whatever decision is made will be the most "rational" though. Rather, Masochist personality only means that they prefer to think through scenarios, following every possibility, before acting. Much like the Sadist, the Masochist has also been misunderstood. He is not in any way cold or malicious. In fact, Masochists very much so look for approval. This is why he works so hard to be rational. He doesn't want to appear "soft" and will often hide behind sarcasm to save face.

CONSTRUCTORS: are completely focused on money and building. They care so much about social status that they often forget to take care of themselves. Often, Constructors bald very young and have potbellies. They eat fast food and microwave dinners because they don't have time to cook. 88% of Constructors have either colon cancer or a stroke before the age of 62.

DE-CONSTRUCTORS: are more esoteric. They would spend more time molding a perfect sphere out of clay than building a skyscraper. They are focused on beauty, but not their own. They often look extremely sloppy and disheveled, but they are never overweight. De-Constructors are extremely conscious of everything they put in their body.

RESULTS: Sadly, because of your inability to properly complete the test, we have been unable to tabulate your personality type without a sizable margin of error. As such, please know that you should have four of the previous eight personality types. For all practical purposes, you may choose the ones that most closely fits your own conception of your personality type, but honestly, if you can't properly take a multiple choice test, chances are, you can't find yourself anyways so really, you should just randomly pick. Also, please remember that it is your own fault for improperly taking *Personality Indicator Version 8.0* that we are unable to yield proper results and that most people are correctly assessed without difficulty, but you managed to fail at even this simple task. *Personality Indicator Version 8.0* is not responsible in any way for your shortcomings and waive all liability. If you feel you have reached this message in error, please feel free to sign up for the *Personality Indicator* again, and thank you once again for your time.

Being as interested in music as the he was
in mathematics, Pythagoras meddled with
the 7 notes of the octave, experimenting with
tones and half-tones, going as far as quarter-

tones, listening for the minor differences one
expression can have against another.

The moon changes phases every 7 days.

chapter

7

: medicating

7

Mother is diabetic. Mother comes from a country that is not so rich as this one. She isn't used to the decadent food. Her body doesn't know how to break it down.

BioVan

Mother calls me, and she says, I have diabetes.

I say, I don't really even know what diabetes is.

She says, Neither do I, but I have medicine for it.

All too often, doctors don't explain conditions. They don't say obvious things like, If you cut down the amount of red meat you eat, it may help your condition. They don't say things like, If you ate less fatty foods, your health would improve. So Mother keeps her diet exactly the same and takes medicine.

My parents are sick. They're old and sick. I have a hard time dealing with this, so for the most part, I try to pretend that it isn't real. My mother is fatalistic. She's constantly reminding me how this time that I see them may be the last time for me to form memories. This is a translation, of course. She wouldn't say something like that in English. She doesn't think she knows how.

My parents aren't really sick. They are and they aren't. My parents are recovering from sickness, and through recovery, they're trying to prevent future sickness. I ask my mother about the medications they're taking. I ask her to list them all for her. I'm surprised she's only taking three. I tell her I want to write an essay about it. She lists them to me.

I ask her, You're only taking three pills?

She says, Yes, but last year, I was taking at least thirty different medicines at the same time. Do you want me to list those for you too?

I say, I think that would be helpful.

She's silent. I hear her ruffling through their three drawers of medication. Even before they were sick, they had an extraordinary medicine collection. It may be because she's a hoarder.

She says, Honey, I think I threw them out.

I'm shocked. I don't say anything.

medicating

She explains, I didn't want to get confused, and you know that whole time was just horrible for me, but I didn't complain, did I? You see? Vietnamese people are stronger than all other kinds of people. Our people know pain, and we can endure it.

My parents are martyrs. They like to remind me of their pain and sacrifice all the time.

She says, My baby, I threw them all away. I'm sorry. Can you do your little project without it?

I say, Of course, but you're really only taking three medications?

She says, You know I've been clean for more than a year now. I don't have to take anything, I just have to go in every three months for a colonoscopy.

She says, Oh will you be sure to mention that I'm having my eyes operated on this month? Both of them. I'm practically blind, you know.

She says this while she's talking on a cell phone while driving.

Mother hates that I study myths, but she revels in the idea that my research can be immortalized on paper. Mother wishes I was in medical school or even law school. Hell, she'd be ok if I was an engineer. Still, she loves it when my name appears on paper. She never reads it of course. She says that her English isn't good enough to understand it. I know that's bullshit, but I let my family get away with a lot. As the youngest, it's required that I accept the faults of everyone older than me. As the youngest, I can essentially be treated like shit.

Biovan is an insulin-mimetic compound. It's still in a pre-clinical trial period. Supposedly, this compound could act as a replacement for insulin. Diabetic patients could live a life without injections if this medicine is approved.

My mother is a guinea pig, but she accepts this without question. My parents don't want to admit it, but we're poor. They'll do about anything to save a few pennies here and there. Also, even nurses can't find Mother's veins to give her injections. Back when she was in chemo, before she had the Mediport put in, she came home with black bruises on her arms. Even though I criticize my mother, I'm proud of her. She endures a lot of pain, and she's incredibly strong.

Father's also diabetic. He's been diabetic for years though. Long before Mother declared that she was diabetic, he had a blood sugar testing kit. The one he has today is much more sophisticated. You'd think that I'd know more about this disease since both my parents have it, but I'm so scared of confronting their sickness that I really do avoid it as much as possible. Even learning what medications they take is overwhelming.

Actos

Actos is a once-a-day pill for people with type 2 diabetes that when added to a healthy diet and regular exercise can aid the body make more effective use of its natural insulin or artificial insulin. This medication helps reduce insulin resistance.

When I was a little girl, Mother came up to me and she looked confused. The mother of my memory is beautiful. She skin is smooth and tan. She's always smiling. Mother came up to me and she said, I don't know why I can't remember this but are there sixty pennies in a dollar or one hundred? I laughed. It wasn't a jovial laugh. It was a mean and bitter laugh, a mocking laugh. I didn't even answer the question. I ran around the house telling everyone how stupid my mom could be. Mother always did things like this. She still does. She gets details confused, swaps characteristics of common things.

Caduet

As far back as I can remember, Mother has been a hypochondriac. She was always sick with something. She came up with illnesses that I'd never heard of. She made up cures that most people in America would think is funny. Mother constantly thinks she's having heart attacks or strokes. We don't think this is funny, but we don't take it seriously. When she was diagnosed with cancer, no one in the family wanted to believe it. We wanted this to be another one of her strange make-believe sicknesses, but it wasn't. It was real, and it was painful to watch. Mostly, Mother was afraid of losing her hair. It seems stupidly superficial, but I think it's a fairly natural reaction. When confronted with something of that magnitude, I don't think I'd want to consider survival statistics or the medical process. I think I'd want to concentrate on hair loss too. Luckily, the kind of treatment she had didn't have hair loss as a side-effect. She'd come home from treatment, skinny, her face and hands black, and she'd cook dinner, and we'd talk, and I'd pretend it wasn't real. When she did complain, it was vague. She didn't want me to be worried. I didn't want her to be sick.

Mother's two characteristics function in different ways, but added together, they create a vital part of her personality. Caduet is a single pill that combines Norvasc and Lipitor. Norvasc lowers blood pressure and Lipitor lowers cholesterol. Mother shouldn't have high blood pressure or high cholesterol, but she does, and she takes one pill to lower both these things.

Father wears sunglasses. I don't visit home often and he doesn't visit me often, it's impractical, but when I do see him, he's always wearing *Lotrel* sunglasses. I don't know when I started noticing that he wore sunglasses inside, but I remember that I was embarrassed by it. I remember that I thought it made him stand out because no one wears sunglasses inside.

I remember my senior recital. Like so many Asian-Americans, I played the violin. I am, in many ways, the stereotypical Asian-American girl. In high school, I played both violin and piano, I was vice-president of student counsel and National Honor Society. I took more math and science courses than would ever be necessary for anyone in high school. I was an over-achiever. I worked hard and got great grades. I didn't have boyfriends, even though I wanted them. I was awkward and my friends weren't the cool kids at the school. I was caught somewhere between wanting to assert my sexuality and respecting my parents enough to try to deny it, but my senior recital. The orchestra conductor only let one student play a solo during the last concert of the year. Rightfully, my best friend Laura and I should both have had the chance to play, but I was Concert Master so I got to play. I played the first movement of Wieniawki's second violin concerto. Father sat in the front row, with his camcorder and his sunglasses. I know he was proud, but I was embarrassed.

Back when I was in high school, I didn't know why my father wore his tinted glasses everywhere. It made him look poor. It hid his eyes in a way that told people that he was embarrassed of himself, that he couldn't even make eye contact with others. It was another layer of shame. One day, Father and I were talking about our family. It isn't often that we have a real conversation and I revel in the opportunity to move beyond the comfort of school or football. Father tells me about his life and his struggles, about how my siblings have disappointed his expectations, how he's scared for my mother and how sick she gets. I hadn't seen it before, but my father wore his sunglasses so I couldn't see him cry. Asian men are emasculated enough through the media. He wouldn't want to be seen as sensitive. Every time Father takes me to the airport, he wears his sunglasses.

I can't imagine the kind of pressure or stress a person goes through trying to suppress emotions on a daily basis. A couple years ago, I found out that both my parents were on anti-depressants. My father takes sleeping pills. It's overwhelming, and I know that they don't talk to each other about it. In Vietnamese, there isn't a word for depressed. The closest words are very sad, which couldn't equate the emotions of a man who has lost his strength, his ability to do simple things, his method of expression. Very sad is an inadequate way of describing an undeniably mundane life, surviving day by day only because the body won't just die, but Father doesn't want to die. He wants to see me be a doctor. He wants to see his dream manifest so he takes his medicine. I'm afraid he doesn't want it bad enough. He's a stubborn man, and although he's willing to take medicine, he isn't willing to change his diet or exercise. He just takes a pill.

Lotrel is a combination of two blood pressure medications: Norvasc and an ACE inhibitor. Norvasc is a calcium channel blocker. Norvasc is a component of Mother's medication as well. The ACE inhibitor prevents the formulation of angiotensin II. Angiotensin I has no negative affect on blood pressure, but sometimes, angiotensin I will turn into angiotensin II, which is bad, and the ACE inhibitor is an enzyme to prevent this transformation.

These are big words, but really, if he would just diet and exercise, I wouldn't need to worry about the long-term affects of all these medications. These are patches to fix problems on a short-term basis, but Father doesn't seem to care about that at all.

It's an issue of privacy. It's also an issue of body image. After Father had his stroke, he had a catheter attached to his urinary tract for almost a year. He couldn't urinate. Four years later, he still has a urinary tract infection. He's had it since he had the catheter removed. I couldn't imagine how helpless it feels to not even be able to piss on your own. I couldn't imagine being male and having a catheter inserted and removed with regularity. I couldn't imagine how painful it is, but more importantly, I couldn't imagine how it makes a person feel, much less my father, a private man, private about everything, exposing his penis for a nurse to shove a tube up so that all the fluid can drain from his bladder. Even now, when he pees, a small percentage of urine is not relieved, and that small amount, maybe an ounce or two, makes his doctors consider having a permanent catheter put in.

Macrobid

A couple months ago, my parents came up to visit me. It was strange, having them in my territory. They were here to attend my graduation, or at least, they called it my graduation. They actually came up to see me present at a conference, which they knew, but up until they were in the building, half an hour before it was set to begin, they asked if I was sure that I wouldn't want them to go to my graduation instead. This was frustrating, but I'm used to it. I said, You know that you're not going to my graduation, and my mother said, But graduations are so much easier for me to understand. She said, You know our English isn't very good, and I said, Mom, this is important to me. I've been doing research on Atlas for years, this is my life. Besides, I'm not even graduating so I don't know what you're expecting anyways. She said, Oh. My father continued to smoke his pipe.

While they were here, I took them to Chicago and Michigan. To play. In Vietnamese, the word for going out and having fun is also the same word for play. It shows that Vietnamese people equate fun with childishness. Adults don't play. They work.

In Michigan, my mother ate something that didn't agree with her body. We had to stop on the way to the lake for her to defecate. She had enough experience to bring napkins with her for this kind of emergency. We stopped four more times during our thirty-minute drive. When we got back into town, we stopped at the Vietnamese grocery store. I went in with my mother and my boyfriend. Father insisted on staying outside to smoke his pipe. Father had been shaky all day, and I didn't want him to be outside alone, still, I didn't stop him.

We shopped. After about ten minutes, I saw Father come into the store. Because Friday is fresh produce day, the store was filled with people. It's a small store. It's hard to fit a person and a cart across the width of an aisle. I'm overprotective with my father, the way he used to be of me when I was a little girl. I saw him, and I pushed my way to him, wanting to hold his arm while he walked. He asked for the bathroom. I showed him where it was. I walked him there. I waited for him by the door. He came out with a large wet stain on his slacks. I averted my eyes. I didn't want him to notice that I had noticed. I pretended it wasn't there. It's part of being a daughter.

Macrobid is an anti-biotic used to combat the bacteria that causes urinary tract infections.

I ask Father, Did you sleep well last night? Is the bed comfortable?

I paid for them to stay at Holiday Inn. My sister paid for their plane ticket. My parents don't have a lot of extra money to spend on their travels.

Father says, No.

He puffs on his pipe.

I say, It's cold in the mornings here. You should wear a hat and a coat.

He says, You're wearing a skirt and a t-shirt.

I say, I'm used to it. Please. At least bring it.

We're late. I have class, and we're already late. Both Mother and Father shuffle around. He doesn't bring an extra coat or hat.

Later, when Mother and I are alone, I ask about the hotel again.

She says, Your father can't control his bladder. He wet the bed in the middle of the night. He got up and cleaned it. Then, he slept on the sofa-chair. I didn't even know until this morning. He does that all the time now. That's why he doesn't want to sleep upstairs with me. He doesn't want to ruin the bed, but he's embarrassed about it so I don't mention it.

It's an image I can't get out of my head. My father lying down and his fingers are bloated. They're huge, and I grab hold of them, and I squeeze, and he doesn't react because he can't feel it at all.

Lyrica

When Mother and Father came to visit, on the way back from Chicago, my boyfriend accidentally slammed the door on my father's hand. From the front seats, we both heard some noises, but we didn't know what it was for a good minute. My father was surprisingly gracious about it. He said, Oh it's ok. I can't feel my fingers anyway.

Lyrica treats nerve damage caused by diabetes, but Father had nerve damage from his stroke, and I wonder if his blood sugar is causing more nerve damage.

My sister calls me and asks if I've talked to Father. I'm always worried when anyone asks that because I'm sure that something horrible has happened, I'm the last to know. They don't want me to be worried without reason.

I say that I haven't.

She says, Well, I just wanted to know because I just got Daddy some new clothes for Father's Day and he should've gotten it already, but I just got off the phone with him and he said that he hadn't gotten it, and I was just wondering if he had gotten it.

I say, Wouldn't he tell you if he got it?

She says, Well, I don't know. That's why I'm calling you. Well, anyway, I got him all these clothes because Mommy said he needed new clothes because some medicine he takes has made him gain all this weight. You know he's a size 36 waist? That's the same size as my husband.

Her husband is a big man. My father isn't. I don't believe her.

Are you sure? I ask. Eric's a lot bigger than Daddy.

Well, that's what Mommy said, she says. She says, I hope she's right but if she isn't, I included a receipt so they can return it.

The thing is that this is the second time I've had this exact conversation with my sister. She just doesn't remember it. She regularly calls me and repeats the same story that she told me the day before. I listen and try to sound interested. Also, my sister has a habit of mailing things to me and my parents priority mail. Usually, her gifts are innocuous and kind, but very unnecessary, especially when shipping is factored in. As soon as she mails it off, whoever receives it is bombarded with phone calls, making sure we got it.

A side-effect of Lyrical is sleepiness and weight gain. When Lyrica is taken with Actos, the weight gain is potentially substantial.

I ask my mother, Is he eating a lot more?
     She says, No, it's the medicine. He sleeps all day.
     My father has always been one to take naps. The only effective uses of time are reading, working, studying, practicing an instrument, and taking naps.
     She says, You won't believe this. He sleeps from noon until six. Then, after dinner, I rub his feet, using that acupressure, you know, and he sleeps from midnight until eight in the morning.

A staple for Vietnamese food is the fish sauce. Fish sauce, surprisingly, has very little fish. It's *Coreg* mainly salt. Father avoids salt in every other form, but he dips everything in fish sauce. Mother uses salt alternatives when cooking, but she doesn't read the label that says that the flavoring has salt in it. She's just not using table salt.
     It's not that she doesn't try. She does. Often, Mother makes salads and other watery greens for them to eat for dinner. They don't eat a lot. Everything is haphazardly moderated. Some nights, she'll make papaya salad. Other nights, they'll eat baked fish, but of course, the baked fish is bland so they dip it in fish sauce.

Coreg is used as treatment for hypertension. When coupled with a healthy diet and exercise, this medication should significantly lower blood pressure. Coreg also acts as a preventative for heart attack and stroke. People who are at risk for heart disease should take Coreg.

When we're in Chicago, Mother says, We should go get you a hula hoop. I just bought one. I read in a magazine that they're really good for you, and I think you need to get some exercise.

It's been about three months since we were in Chicago together. Mother says, You know, you should really get a hula hoop. I love mine.

I'm skeptical. I say, Are you?

She says, Yes, but it's hard. You remember that first time I told you about it, I did it for five minutes and then the next day, I tried again, and it just fell off me. I couldn't get it to stay up. So I left it alone for a couple weeks. When I picked it up, I could do it again, and I was so excited I did it for ten minutes. Since then, I haven't been able to and my body's all bruised, but it doesn't hurt.

I ask, Is it supposed to bruise you?

The directions say it's perfectly normal.

I say, Did the directions tell you how long you should hula hoop for the first few times?

She says, Three minutes.

I say, How long did you do it?

Five, she says. She doesn't understand why it hasn't worked for her.

When I was little, I used to wrap my knees and ankles in bandages. Sometimes, if I couldn't find the right kind of bandage, I'd *Celebrex* use a handkerchief or scarf. When my parents asked me what was wrong, I told them I had arthritis. I don't know how I even knew what arthritis was, but I was sure that I had it.

Celebrex relieves arthritis by blocking the enzyme COX-2. COX-2 plays a key role is causing both inflammation and pain. Celebrex is unique from other pain relievers because it only blocks COX-2. Most other painkillers block COX-1 and COX-2. COX-1 protects the lining of the stomach.

I didn't even know my father had arthritis.

Aspirin saved my father's life. That sounds melodramatic, but six months before his stroke, he started taking one aspirin a day. He'd heard it on some nightly news special. When he told me he was taking aspirin, not knowing anything, I told him it was probably bad for him to do it. I thought aspirin was bad for the stomach. I didn't know why I thought this. I probably heard it on some nightly news special. I told him he shouldn't believe everything he hears on TV.

Aspirin

After his stroke, the doctor said his stroke would've been a lot worse if he hadn't taken the aspirin. Now both my parents take aspirin every day.

When I was a little girl, one of my grandmother's friends lived a block away. My grandmother and I would walk over there almost every day, and her friend gave me butter cookies. I loved her. I never knew her husband, but my grandmother told me that he smoked and she nagged him to quit smoking and he did and then he died. My grandmother didn't tell me that it was because he quit smoking that he died, but I think that was the implication. Her friend never forgave herself for killing her husband.

Lipitor

My father has smoked since I've been alive. In my mind, he has three trademarks. The first and most important one is his pipe. Any time he leaves the house, he shuffles around here and there to make sure that he has his pipe and a small pouch of tobacco. Even when I was young, this was annoying, but I've never been able to separate images of pipe and Father.

Since his stroke, Mother's urged him to quit smoking in her passive-aggressive way. Asian women only offer their opinions, she explained to me. Still, he shuffles, slower now than before, around looking for his pouch and pipe. His mind isn't as sharp as before and sometimes, he'll retrace his way through the house several times thinking he'd forgotten something.

His second trademark is that he's always late, usually by half an hour or so. I'm told that this is a Vietnamese thing, but I don't buy it. Even though his being late was bothersome and at times inconvenient, it didn't worry me until recently. Now that Father has so many pills to juggle, if he's late taking one pill, it could completely counter the affect of another one. If Father doesn't eat when he's supposed to, his blood sugar could drop. Father's life is now contingent on his timing, and he's never been good with time.

His last trademark is his belly. When I was a little girl, I'd sit on his belly and call him Winnie-the-Pooh. I didn't watch many cartoons as a child, but I did read all the A. A. Milne books. Winnie was my favorite. I also used to joke that he had a watermelon in his belly. He'd bounce me up and down and I'd giggle. Back then, I didn't know it was unhealthy, I just thought it was funny. I also didn't think that I could have hurt his feelings, but I thought he was invincible, and invincible people don't have feelings to hurt.

Lipitor is a cholesterol-lowering agent for people with Type II diabetes proven to help reduce chance of stroke or heart attack for those with near normal cholesterol, and at least one other risk factor, such as high blood pressure or smoking.

Father didn't go to the doctor for at least a decade. We had insurance. He just didn't want to go. He wouldn't admit this even now, but I'm sure he didn't go because he didn't want to hear everything that was wrong with him. My father is stubborn. He's probably the most stubborn person I've ever met. He didn't want to go to the doctor because he might have to change his lifestyle if he heard that he was unhealthy or his life was in danger. I said, he might. Since he had his stroke, a stroke that could have killed him, a stroke that killed half his body and more, he hasn't actually changed anything about his life. He's handicapped. He isn't as strong as he was, but he hasn't done a damned thing about anything.

I say this because I'm angry. I say this because I'm completely pissed off that he knows that his body has failed him and he knows that if he doesn't change the way he lives in a fundamental way, he's going to die, and if he dies before my mom dies, she'll die pretty soon after he does, and I can't deal with that. Selfishly, I want him to live. I'm not ashamed to admit that. I want my parents to live because I don't want a life without them.

The Pythagoreans loved perfect numbers, and even though they believed that 10 was the most perfect number, they thought that 6 was possibly the second most perfect number. Not only does 1 + 2 + 3 = 6 but also 1 x 2 x 3 = 6. Furthermore, 6 is the product of the first man (3) and the first woman (2), but alas, I am getting ahead of myself.

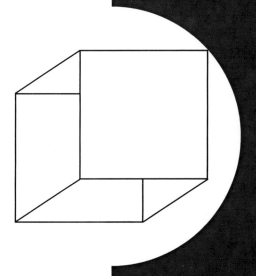

The Pythagoreans also noted 6 is the first number to represent a plane of existence.

The cube is made of 6 sides, and they believed that it is the ideal form for any closed construction.

chapter

6

what he saw

6

In 1823, Reverend Thomas Dick saw fortifications on the moon.

Before Copernicus, astronomers and philosophers saw the earth as the center of the universe.

In 1877, Giovanni Schiaparelli saw "canali" on Mars. Translated into English, "canali" can mean either channel or canal. Given that channels are natural and canals are artificial, Schiaperelli's Italian word was translated to mean canals. It is unclear which word the astronomer would have preferred for his discovery.

To see stellar parallax is to see a change in angular position between two stationary objects or stars. These object don't actually need to be stationary as long as the observer is also moving, as all observers on Earth are. In other words, stellar parallax is the visible shift of an object against the background of another object due to a change in the observer's position.

To astronomers up until the 19th century, stellar parallax was the only way to prove that Copernicus was right.

In 1669, Robert Hooke found stellar parallax in gamma Draconis. It was a huge parallax too, 15″. The search for parallax had been a primary concern to most astronomers since Copernicus shocked the universe into a heliocentric system, which is to say that Hooke was content with his discovery.

In the 1720s, James Bradley discovered that Hooke didn't find the first instance of stellar parallax. Bradley explained that Hooke thought he'd seen the minute shift in the star because he'd forgotten to shift his telescope to account for the earth's annual rotation. Hooke was conned by the aberration of starlight.

In 1907, Karl Bohlin observed Andromeda's stellar parallax. He believed that it was part of the Milky Way and close enough to see its parallax.

Andromeda is an island universe and therefore not a part of the Milky Way.

When Ptolemy looked up at the night, he saw stars stuck to a great spherical vault that hung somewhere beyond the orbit of Saturn.

Immanuel Kant was the first to see that the universe is shaped like a pancake. He thought he had stolen the idea from Thomas Wright based on a review of Wright's newest book. Kant (and the reviewer) misread the book.

Kant also saw his moral laws as universal moral laws, by which he meant that all intelligent beings—terrestrial and extraterrestrial—should obey his philosophies.

William Herschel built big telescopes to sweep the night sky. His monstrous 48-inch-aperture reflecting telescope saw forests, canals, pyramids, and extensive vegetation on the moon. Even as Herschel catalogued the thousands of new nebulae and star clusters he discovered, he dreamt of building bigger telescopes. He wanted a telescope big enough to display Lunarians with clarity.

The symbol signifying stellar parallax angle is the same symbol as inches, but it means arc seconds.

Tycho Brahe estimated that the distance from the earth to the sun was 1,150 earth radii and the distance from the earth to the Saturn was 123,000 radii. This made the ceiling stained with stars roughly 14,000 earth radii away from his telescope.

In 1838, Friedrich Bessel announced that he saw the first true instance of stellar parallax. John Herschel proclaimed that his discovery was the "greatest and most glorious triumph which practical astronomy has ever witnessed."

In 1669, Robert Hooke measured a stellar parallax of 15" in gamma Draconis. In the 1690s, England's Astronomer Royal John Flamsteed saw a 40" parallactic shift in Polaris. Giuseppe Piazzi, a prominent Italian astronomer in the early 1800s, saw parallax in not one but three stars: Aldeberan, Sirius, and Procyon. Fellow Italian D. Calendrelli saw a 4.4" parallactic shift in Vega. John Brinkley, Ireland's Astronomer Royal, had also seen stellar parallax in: Vega, Altair, Arcturus, and Deneb. They all saw optical illusions.

Bessel really did see parallax, and in 1838, the Copernican theory of a heliocentric universe was finally accepted.

Some of his canals were 300 kilometers wide.

In 1795, the Astronomer Royal of Greenwich Observatory fired his assistant for improper seeing. The more technical term would be flawed observational technique. Nevil Maskelyne relieved David Kinnebrooke of his duties for 800 msecs of skewed research. Kinnebrooke, up until his last second of breath in the observatory, swore that his data was accurate. Maskelyne insisted that it didn't match his own observations, thereby making lesser-experienced assistant's wrong.

In 1826, Friedrich Bessel went over this data and found that the observations of both Kinnebrooke and Maskelyne were correct. Bessel discovered what is today known as personal equation, that is, that everyone has a slightly different reaction time to light, and observations must be given a window of error to account for this snapshot discrepancy.

In 1846, Lord Rosse built a behemoth 72-inch-aperture reflecting telescope and through it, he resolved the Orion nebulae. He was sure he could resolve any nebulae. In 1847, William Bond of Harvard University used a 15-inch refracting telescope to verify Rosse's resolution of Orion.

In 1864, William Huggins used spectroscopy to reveal that some nebulae, Orion included, are glowing gases; therefore, they cannot be resolved.

In 1933, Fritz Zwicky looked into the California sky and saw what could not be seen. He saw a swallowing darkness, a darkness that eats light. In 1933, Zwicky theorized that darkness covers other matter. He did not necessarily assume that it unrelentingly consumed, just that it blanketed.

His idea has manifested itself as dark matter. Dark matter distorts close to 95% of what is seen.

On February 18, 1930, Clyde Tombaugh saw a tiny dot move from one point to another while going through January photographic plates. This tiny dot was later named Pluto.

Between 1876 and 1909, many people saw dark spots against the sun's surface. The aberration was named Vulcan. Most hoped it was a new planet. LeVerrier, mathematical co-discoverer of Neptune, was a staunch believer in Vulcan.

The canals made a spider web across Mars, an intricate pattern of straight lines running to and fro, bringing thawed ice to Martians huddled in small huts.

In 1835, *The New York Sun* reported that John Herschel saw Lunarians from his observatory at the Cape of Good Hope. The moon people were described as half-human, half-bat chimeras. They were seen engaging in rational conversations. The moon was also residence to other fantastical creatures such as unicorns and miniature zebras. From the tip of Africa, John Herschel also saw large temples, signifying the Vespertilio-homo's belief in God. Near the Bay of Rainbows, Herschel and his team sighted creatures glowing beyond angelic. They assumed these were the superior forms of Vespertilio-homo.

In 1840, a reporter from *The Journal of Commerce* asked to see Herschel's records. *Sun* reporter Richard Adams Locke revealed that he had written the entire account himself.

Percy Shelley saw stars and suns as hells.

Adriaan van Maanen saw slight shifts in the internal movements of spiral nebulae in 1916 and concluded that spiral nebulae rotate. Using this information, Harlow Shapley strongly argued against the Island Universe Theory in what is now known as the Great Debate. Both Shapley and van Maanen believed that if spiral nebulae rotated at the speed predicted, they could not be island universes, but more importantly, they could not sustain life.

Edwin Hubble re-examined the mathematics and found no evidence to support van Maanen's claim for rotation. Hubble went so far as to exclaim that van Maanen only saw what he expected to see.

In 1915, Einstein published a paper that accounted for the advance of the perihelion of Mercury. He proved that Vulcan cannot exist.

In 1917, Adriaan van Maanen saw a star whiter than all the others he had seen. It wasn't brighter or bigger, just whiter. He couldn't explain it to others, but he did get a star named after him.

Van Maanen's star is a white dwarf. It was the second white dwarf discovered.

By 1883, Schiaparelli observed his canals geminate, or double. He claimed that he couldn't see the gemination before because his telescope had been too weak. By 1884, all telescopes were judged based on their ability to resolve this phenomenon.

Of course, Pluto isn't even a planet anymore.

On March 13, 1781, William Herschel saw either a curious object that he thought could be either a nebulous star or a comet. Even after trustworthy professionals told him it was most likely a planet, he insisted it was a comet. Even after comet expert Messier explained to him that it couldn't be a comet because it lacked comet-like traits, William Herschel remained steadfast in his belief that he found another comet. After much hard-headedness, in June 1782, he finally called the object "my planet" and wanted to name it Georgium Sidus after King George III.

This comet is what is now known as Uranus.

In "Essay of Man," Alexander Pope wrote:

> *Superior beings, when of late they saw*
> *A mortal man unfold all Nature's law,*
> *Admired such wisdom in an earthly shape*
> *And shewed a Newton as we shew an Ape.*

Pope did not need to see an extraterrestrial to portray him.

In 1844, Ellen White had a vision. She counted the moons of Jupiter and gave majestic descriptions of the rings of Saturn. Then, she spoke of the people who lived on Saturn. She saw their purity and beauty, a glowing cleanliness that Earthlings lacked. She saw a world without sin. The Saturnians were extremely tall, she said.

Ellen White was the main prophetess and co-founder of the Seventh-day Adventists.

Uranus was seen at least 23 times before its discovery in 1781.

During a time when belief in plurality was at its height, William Whewell spoke out against it. During a time when people believed that God would not waste His time on creating heavens without populating them, William Whewell studied the undeniable facts of Geology, and from this, he surmised that if Geology was correct in asserting that the Earth was billions of years old and humans were not, then God was wasteful with Time, and if God could be wasteful with an atom of time, why not an atom of space. William Whewell shook plurality.

Still, when William Whewell looked up into the heavens, he saw that Jupiter was populated with fish people, beings not as evolved as humans, but they couldn't be because Jupiter wasn't even a solid planet. Rather, their planet was composed of a viscous liquid, and any beings on that planet would need to have been cartilaginous and glutinous masses. His fish people had no hands.

what he saw

Most believed that the canals were used as irrigation systems. Schiaparelli said he saw vegetation along the edges of the canals.

In 1876, Richard Proctor saw that planets, like humans, go through an aging or evolutionary process. By looking around our own solar system, we could unravel the entire universe. The first stage is the youthful stage, where planets burst energetic flames of hydrogen and helium. Richard Proctor compared this to our sun. The second stage surges great heat but lacks the display of bright lights. Proctor claimed that Saturn and Jupiter vivify this phase. The third stage shows less heat and less light. It isn't a spectacular evolutionary moment, but it is the condition of the Earth, a mediocre blink in planetary life. Finally, there is the stage that signifies the decay of both heat and light, a metaphorical sigh in remembrance of fireworks and playfulness. This is the where is the moon is, our moon. Richard Proctor describes it as planetary decrepitude.

He believed that life could be supported only during the earthlike phase. The first two stages are too hot and the last too cold.

It's not certain that he believed in an apocalyptic future, but it would seem that Richard Proctor did believe in plurality.

Proctor was a principle popularizer of modern astronomy.

Joseph Smith was the First Prophet, Seer, and Revelator of the Church of Jesus Christ of Latter-day Saints. He saw visions of angels living on distant planets but governing Earth.

This was not included in the *Book of Mormon*. Perhaps that was a wise idea.

Ralph Waldo Emerson resigned his position as pastor because he couldn't reconcile his beliefs with the administration of the Lord's Supper. He believed in astronomy. He saw that the revelations of astronomy can force any thinking person to reject not only atheism but of also the fundamentals of Christianity, particularly the notion of divine incarnation and redemption.

Emerson once questioned that given the developments of modern astronomy, who can be a Calvinist or who an Atheist?

Percival Lowell was a wealthy man. He became so excited by the Canals of Mars that he built an observatory to see the amazing canals himself. Lowell Observatory housed a 24" refracting telescope, and through that telescope, Lowell saw geminations.

According to Bode's Law, there should be a planet in rotation between Mars and Jupiter. On January 1, 1801, Giuseppe Piazzi saw sign of the planet. By January 14, it started to move. By February, it was no longer visible, and few believed Piazzi's claim that he'd found the missing planet. Karl Friedrich Gauss, a young and brilliant mathematician, saved the day by charting the planet's hypothetical position based off of Piazzi's observations. December 31, 1801, Piazzi sighted the planet once again and named it Ceres.

Ceres is located in what is today known as the asteroid belt. It is the largest and most prominent asteroid.

Clyde Tombaugh discovered Pluto at Lowell Observatory.

In 1947, residents in New Mexico saw strange lights flashing from an abnormal flying structure. On June 14, William Brazel finds abnormal bits of debris on his farm.

People now take pilgrimages to Roswell.

It was not until 1894 that someone suggested that the Canals of Mars might be an optical illusion. This someone was E. Walter Maunder. He was, for the most part, ignored.

When the Atomists looked up at the Heavens, they saw something homogenous but infinite, stars randomly thrown onto a never-ending canvas, a universe without purpose. When Aristotle and his followers extended their gaze upwards, they saw the opposite of what the Atomists saw. The exact opposite.

In 1903, E. Walter Maunder published the results of an experiment. A group of schoolboys were shown a picture of Mars without canals but with the appropriate topographical features. They were asked to replicate the drawing freehand and at various distances. They all drew canals.

In 1277, Etienne Tempier, Bishop of Paris, became concerned that too many theologians, Thomas Aquinas in particular, saw the universe the way the Aristotelians had. As such, Bishop Tempier decreed the Condemnation of 1277, which contained 217 propositions and anyone who believed any of these propositions was threatened with excommunication.

Tempier feared that theologians had rationalized God's powers to such an extent that they put limitations on His abilities. Proposition 34 states "that the first cause [God] could not make several worlds."

In 1608, Galileo Galilei saw the Heavens as the Heavens had never been seen before. In 1608, Galileo made minor adjustments to his seeing machine and raised his newly invented telescope to crystallize images of night. Through this mechanical invention, he made sensational discoveries. Among these were: that the moon has both mountains and oceans; that Jupiter has four moons orbiting it; and that there are many more stars than had ever been seen or imagined.

Galileo did not use these discoveries to prove or disprove plurality.

Isaac Newton saw that a 200-pound earthling would weigh at least twice that amount on Jupiter and twenty-three times that on the Sun.

Benjamin Franklin once wrote, "I believe there is one Supreme most perfect Being, author and father of the gods themselves. For I believe that man is not the most perfect Being but one, but rather that there are many degrees of beings superior to him."

Auguste Comte, founder of Positivism, believed that one should only study what can be seen and, therefore, known.

In 1909, Eugene Antoniadi fully resolved Mars. There were no canals. Slowly, the world came to accept that the infamous Canals of Mars were merely an optical illusion.

Alfred Russell Wallace, co-discoverer of evolution, staunchly argued against plurality. Among the principles of evolution are chance and time, and the possibility of the exact series of mutations that brought forth sentient beings on Earth being replicated elsewhere is beyond impossible. Wallace saw plurality in the most practical manner.

In 1913, Antoniadi wrote, "Ponderous volumes will still be written to record the discovery of new canals. But the astronomer of the future will sneer at these wonders; and the canal fallacy, after retarding the progress of astronomy for a third of a century, is doomed to be relegated into the myths of the past."

Reverend Thomas Dick cited the population of the Saturn's rings to be 8,141,963, 826, 080.

The Pythagoreans saw that man is made of good and evil, and like man, the number 5 is made of good (odd) and bad (even).

They thought that 5 was a circular number, always beginning and ending with itself, never moving beyond its starting point.

chapter

5

news:
(march 02, 2005)

5

Today is March the second, two thousand five, but the date itself is arbitrary, hardly even important, although in all actuality, it's quite important, but not to you, not to any of you, but it's important to me which is to say that I don't believe that anyone cares about that which is arbitrary even if that which is arbitrary is to me rather important, but surely this is unimportant so surely, as they say, I should stop this rambling if only momentarily. Of course, I feel that it is of the greatest importance that I inform you, any of you, that today is March the second, two thousand five, and I am reading *The New York Times* and indeed I read *The New York Times* every day. It is perhaps, how to say, a tendency of mine to read this fine newspaper daily and sit daily at this fine café and drink fine coffee poured by the most lovely of Turk's caps, and she is perhaps certainly the most lovely of all Turk's caps if indeed I have ever seen a Turk's cap although if truth is truth, I have never to my knowledge ever seen a true Turk's cap that isn't my chirping little waitress.

And so here I sit in the New Buffalo Café reading my *New York Times* and drinking my coffee and perching after my Turk's cap. Of course I am positively certain that you wonder why I tell you any of this, and if truth is truth, I must confess that I haven't the most small of ideas. I feel as though clarification is implied for a statement such as this, you see, I am a man and I am a man that has been hardened and I have a lack of belief in the kindness of mankind by which I do infer that man is not kind and man does not care about man, much less a man such as myself, although I do insist that I care about man even if he cares not for me. This of course makes it obvious why I am indeed writing, but in the opportunity that you have a negative amount of creativity, I will indeed clarify that I am writing this because it is a tendency of mine to sit at this café reading this newspaper watching this fine specimen of woman pour coffee, but mainly, I am a collector of fine photographs from this newspaper. Perhaps you believe that it is a derivative of boredom that causes this sort of excessive word usage, but indeed, I am a collector of pictures, but I am, as they say, more than that in that not only do I collect them by removing them from the paper itself but I am also a reproducer of these fine photographs. I find it needed to confess to you because mainly I am a man of honesty that I am not a professional reproducer.

I am a man who does very little. You see I have never been, as they say, employed in my life and I am positive that you question the practicality of a man of my age and certainly my stature to have never been employed. Indeed, even I see it as overly impractical, but truth being truth, I find it needed here to confess my secrets. You see, many years ago, I was working on my doctorate. It indeed must have been so many years previous to this year that I can hardly remember what I was studying, but I am certain that it must have been something that was quite interesting. But as I was explaining, I was completing my graduate work, and indeed, I was most concerned that I would be unable to support my style of living once I completed my work as I had, even at that nascent age, never been employed. My mind being so occupied as it was, I found the only solution to relieve my head from its overpowering suffrage was to masturbate. So I was in my apartment masturbating and considering my options for the future when I received a knock on my door. Indeed even then I was unaccustomed to visitors so when a visitor of sorts did appear, I myself became quite excited and simply by hearing a visitor inquire my name sufficed as catalyst for me to, as they say, complete the assignment in my hand.

And thus completing and wiping from my penis the excess semen, I quickly adorned my body with clothing to properly answer the knocking still present at my door. Two men in suits stood before me. They were both fair enough to look at, and I was momentarily disappointed that my assignment had already been completed, and even as they spoke, I eagerly looked to a time in the future that I could again, as they say, masturbate. Of course, this effervescent infatuation quickly subsided when I realized why these attractive men were visiting me.

I feel it is needed at this time to elaborate if only briefly. You see, at this moment I was bestowed with a family, and although if truth be truth, I hardly cared for them, with the exception of my smaller sister whom was, as they say, full of sprite and energy. I must also divulge at this moment that my lovely little Turk's cap also has this strangeness in her, and it is my belief that this is why she is to me so fascinating, but alas, this is not the time for me to elaborate on my inherent desires. It is not a rarity that I become unfocused, but indeed, I was telling you about my family. You see, my family had long ago developed a habit of traveling to less than traditional vacation destinations, not that they were necessarily undesirable places, only that they were a touch abnormal, if you will. This year, which was the year that I was, as they say, enveloped in my studies, my family traveled to the heat of New Mexico to appreciate the various specimens of cacti.

This, of course, is the moment that things become, as they say, negative. You see, these two rather attractive men came knocking on my front door as I was eagerly stroking my erect penis to tell me that my entire family had, as they say, been killed, by which I mean that not only had my parents died but also my smaller sister and my other siblings of which I hardly recall. It was not a regular occurrence for men like this to make house calls, you see, but indeed mine was an extraordinary circumstance.

The men came to my door to tell me the story of my family's method of decay, by which I intend to say that they were at the door to tell me how my family was killed. Indeed, these incredibly pleasantly aesthetic men informed me that my family was returning home from New Mexico without difficulty when somewhere near the Arizona border ten convicts ran before their minivan. You see, these ten convicts had only recently escaped from the penitentiary by method of tunnel digging, and these men only recently liberated were eager to, as they say, stretch their wings. So these men so full of the adrenaline of escape ran across the highway that happened to be the very same highway that my family was driving on. If truth be truth, I must confess that at this moment, my mouth was agape with anticipation because these men had not completed the story of my family's demise. You see, my mother who happened to be driving the minivan had the reflexes of a chicken as she was, as they say, born in the year of a chicken. Now I am sure that you are skeptical that chickens have ample reflexes, but let me promise you that they do. I myself attest to the truth that chickens are quick on their legs.

Of course, I have again strayed away from the story. Let me return as the story is nearly complete. As I was standing in the doorway half unclothed and increasingly excited if only visually, these men told me that my mother managed to not harm any of these escapees. In fact, the minivan stopped only inches from them. If this is not incredible enough for you, let me continue. The men went on to tell me that my family was utterly unharmed by this occurrence but they were in a condition of shock. Of course, the prisoners were shocked as well, and as both parties, and in my mind they were parties in their own manner, were shocked, neither group heard the song of the siren nearing. You see, simultaneous to this very strange occurrence, two men had robbed a convenience store and three police cars were eagerly chasing them as they had shot and very nearly killed one of the store employees. I am told by these men that the employee was rather attractive, I believe the word they used was foxy, but I wouldn't wager a large sum of money on that particular word, if truth be truth. Of course, it matters not if she was attractive or even if she was female at all. What I ought to be most concerned with was that the two men sped down the highway, the very same highway on which my family and the escaped convicts were silently shocked, and that these two robbers also had the instincts of chickens and managed to circumvent both the prisoners and the minivan, but the three police cars that followed quickly on their bumpers did not.

To very efficiently sum up this tale, my entire family was killed when three police cars consecutively intersected with the minivan. I am told that there was a large explosion of sorts, but I am unsure if this was just a kind of elaboration. Of course, this doesn't quite explain the men, but I am quickly moving to this. You see, these men, who I can't stress how very good looking they were, these men stood in my very small doorway to offer me a lifetime allowance of five thousand dollars per month for the unfortunate death of entire family from the New Mexico government. Now I must divulge that I had never heard of such an odd thing, but of course, my entire family had also never been killed before. I should not find it necessary to speak that I accepted the money and the money has always arrived without entanglements.

And you see? Is it readily obvious to you how easily I am led down tedious paths that relate very little to the present state of things? I am now unsure how it is even possible that I have indeed divulged so much of my history to you when it was simply my intention to mention my current fancy, which of course is to produce reproductions of the magnificent photographs displayed in *The New York Times*. Indeed, I do spend the entirety of my days sitting here in the New Buffalo Café watching my pleasant little Turk's cap run around in her lovely little light green skirt flittering coffee into my cup as I read and reproduce. Oh and I remember oh how I remember the first time she spoke to me. I hope that it is not too inconvenient for me at this moment to reminisce if only for a short while.

Well you see I am no stranger to this city, and it may well be stated with boldness that I am from this very city in which I now sit, and I had long established that I was more than familiar with every interesting location that allows citizens to sit and locute with other interesting citizens. Of course, being as convinced as I was, it was, as they say, a shock when I found the New Buffalo Café. It was perhaps the most enjoyable of shocks, particularly when I chose a table, I have hence learned that it is table c5, and saw the most lovely of creations walk towards me with a pot of black coffee. She looked at me and almost in retarded motion, she shut her right eyelid and shot me a small smile, and it was then it was that moment that I confirmed that she is truly lovely.

Of course, infatuation can only grow when watered with kind words, and my little Turk's cap curved her back to bring her body, oh yes her body I've yet to even describe the fantasy her body can create, closer to my own pathetic body, and her eyes engaged mine in a momentary conversation. It was after this brief conversation that the most amazing of occurrences occurred, and she, my beautiful Turk's cap, she spoke! Yes, I know it is more than impossible to believe that someone as perfect as her, virtually a goddess radiating through the shell of her bones, could speak, but I assure you that I speak truth, and if truth be truth, she looked upon me and she said, Would like some café, Herr Doktor? The sweetness of sound! Yes, she spoke, and like a fool so foolish I replied, Yes, I would, my little Turk's cap. And that was indeed the story as it stands. That was the first interaction I had with my Turk's cap in this the New Buffalo Café, and I have appeared in this very seat every day since that first day.

Now I feel it necessary once again to clarify a tiny detail or two. You see, from that first day, I was small amount perplexed because you see, ever since that first day, my Turk's cap has called me Herr Doktor, which in itself is hardly problematic only that I am not German and neither is she. Of course, I should not need to verbalize this but the irony is impossible to bypass in such a manner. You see, if truth be truth, I don't even speak a word of German! What furthers this humor is that she doesn't either! I must divulge more of my secrets now that I have begun. You see, it is that my Turk's cap and I were introduced with such, how to say, yes, pet names that I have since then never engaged enough courage to forthrightly inquire her true name.

I have often spoken to a doctor friend of mine about this. You see, I am a man of less than pure health. Please do not be concerned, although I doubt you, any of you, have the altruism to care much less be even slightly concerned about me, but surely, I wouldn't want your pity either. I suppose it would be most unpleasurable for me to consider that I have guilted you into caring for me when if truth is truth, I hardly care whether you would care even if in fact you did care. But of course, all of this caring has little to do with my doctor friend, who I must confess that if truth is truth, he is truthfully a doctor and not only is he a doctor, making him a very positive member of our, how to say, society, but certainly the most important quality of my doctor friend is that he cares about me. Please, I plead to you not to interpret this inappropriately. There is certainly nothing out of the ordinary is my relationship with my dear doctor friend, other than of course, that he cares for me in a world that truthfully has such small amounts of care for me.

Now then my doctor friend, I must confess that he was once my physician. It was not until he and I had a, how to say, spiff that the two of us became united as comrades. You see, recently, I arrived at my designated appointment and my physician, please understand that he was certainly not my friend at this point, was pointedly tardy, and most obviously I don't have a, how to say, tight schedule, but I was certainly, as any person would be, bothered by his lateness. Of course, the story hardly ends here. You see, not only was he late, but when he arrived, he also had the gall to inform me that it was absolutely needed that I take some time from work in order to rest and relax because he could tell that I was overly stressed from an excess of labor.

Of course, I could not accept something so ridiculous as this! I have, of course, already spoken the tale of how obviously impossible my doctor friend's diagnosis was. It was this moment that I realized how absolutely subjective the medical profession was that united me with my doctor, and it was this very second that I determined myself to never again enter a doctor's office, but then I was also sure that this man would be a permanent friend of mine.

As upset as I became, I must confess yet again that although I reacted with such violence and vengance at my doctor friend, I did indeed take his advice. You see, ever since I visited him that fateful day, I have since then returned to the New Buffalo Café every day to, as they say, rest and relax. Every day, I sit at this one table and watch my beautiful Turk's cap wisp to and fro bringing to customers coffee with blooming smiles. Even now as I sit here composing this piece and crafting pictures that mirror the photographs displayed in *The New York Times*, I am fully relaxed because my darling Turk's cap is near.

Indeed, I am certain that you question whether or not it is potential that I may retain stillness when my Turk's cap is not near. To this, I reply that indeed when I am separated from my Turk's cap, my existence is not so joyous. In fact, I have often considered speaking with my physician friend about this ailment, but I am positive that he will react poorly to it. You see, I have on occasion spoken to him about her, and constantly, he informs me that my infatuation with her is not natural, which most certainly, this is problematic to me. But of course, you see it is not because I am so much older than her that he thinks is unnatural, although if truth be truth, I am a seasoned man of thirty and I doubt that she can be a second older than twenty. My doctor friend has urged me on more than one occasion that it is needed that I should divest my deepest emotions to her. He insists that to not tell of love is the worst of punishments, worse even than that of Atlas with the weight of denser weight ever known, but to my doctor friend, certainly, to not relieve love is a weight much more painful.

If truth is truth, I must confess that it is a terrible punishment, this weight of loving her without her knowledge. Even last night, I must confess that I had a dream that my lovely Turk's cap  agreed to join me at a cocktail party, and if truth is truth, I would never ask someone I respect and adore to the limit that I adore and respect her to an outing so terrible as a cocktail party, but of course, dreams are entities entirely of themselves, but even then, I have long established that cocktail parties are nothing more than breeding grounds for inappropriate activities. To think that I would even desire my Turk's cap to sit around drinking a cocktail and nervously chatter about how absolutely marvelous everyone else looks. Of course, this would be a lie to everyone but my Turk's cap. Indeed, in my dream, I opened the door to the house in which the cocktail party was being held, and she sashayed into the room with that lovely blue dress on, and all the people were silenced at her grace and beauty. In fact, the party was hardly laborious or tedious because of her presence. I must confess, if truth is truth, that I woke up smiling despite the fact that my semen had exploded entirely on my sheets. Indeed, there was so much semen that I am not entirely sure that it came from just one ejaculation.

But I most definitively would not want you to believe that all of my dreams about my darling and pure Turk's cap are so promiscuous as the one I previously described. If truth is truth, I most tell you that most regularly, they are in totality completely innocuous. Most regularly, my dreams are images, most similar to the photographs exhibited in *The New York Times*. It is not rare when the images I've replicated from *The New York Times* appear in my dreams, only my dear Turk's cap's face is inserted instead of some other person's face. I remember I had this one dream in particular that had my darling Turk's cap and myself in a city quite foreign to this one. I am most sure that it was a changed city because of the strange architecture and brick streets. At the time, I was certain we were somewhere in central Europe, but of this I am now not as positive.

What was most strange about this image that strikes me even today was that her face was blurred but indeed I could tell that we were having the most marvelous of vacations. You see, her face is downcast, shy like a chicken. Now I am certainly positive that you doubt my accuracy of chickens being shy, but let me assuage your concerns because I have extensive understanding about the nature of chickens and I am more than positive that chickens are by nature, how to say, girlishly shy. If you approach one, she will run off and certainly, no proper chicken will allow you to pick her up, much less ruffle her feathers. Only poorly bred chickens would allows atrocities as I've described.

For me to speak of atrocities reminds me of a most humorous anecdote, and I believe that even you, yes you, you uncaring people out there, will find it, how to say, amusing. You see, when I was a small boy, I was afflicted with, how to say, a liar's bug. No, that isn't quite it, but I'm quite assured that you understand what I am intending to mean, but of course, please do not interpret this wrongly. You see, as a small boy, I had very seldom friends, and it was an urge for companionship that brought about this ill habit of telling small falsehoods. Indeed, I am an honest man! Even though I did once tell many fibs, they were small fibs that hurt certainly not one person at all, but of course, these non-truths are the purpose of this quick tale for you.

As a small boy, I wanted other students to think I was from a, how to say, strange land. I would tell my comrades that I came from a small village on Lake Titicaca, which was a lake I made up using my most favorite letters in the alphabet. I would tell my fellow students the most fabulous stories about this town, and with each story, I developed  more and more bonds with other small children, and if truth is truth, I was most happy then. Of course, you must know by now that in eventuality, things such as this do not end with joy. So in truth I had gained many friends, and

I was a popular boy. I had even acquired a young lady to hang upon my arm. Once a week she allowed me the pleasure to kiss any place on her body. I blush now to even consider telling you the many pleasurable things we did together, but indeed, as things did occur, it was this girl who uncovered my lies to my newly made friends. You see, I had told my classmates that Lake Titicaca was in Venezuela, but in fact, one day this girlfriend of mine examined a map only to reveal that Lake Titicaca did indeed exist, a great shock to me!, and that it was positioned in Bolivia. I should hardly need to articulate how I have never since that time had a positive dream about this girl. In fact, if truth is truth, I feel that I must confess that she was the last lover I've had in my life. You see, it is not that I am frightened, but if truth is truth, I simply cannot allow another person to enter so near my weak heart only to destroy it in such a, dare I say, heartless manner.

My doctor friend indeed has often spoken to me about this. You see, he is quite concerned with my overall health if I have never, how to say, mated. I am sure you understand. It is not as though I lack the urges to do so, but the memory of the pain that evil girl inflicted on me is too difficult to ignore. It should not be thought of as ironic that her name was Lilith. Oh! If only my little Turk's cap could be named Eve. She would be perfection after the tainted horror and latent evil emanating from the memory of Lilith and that nightmarish time in my life.

But most certainly my doctor friend has been very kind in listening to my tales. He is my most favorite companion, other than my darling Turk's cap of course. Just earlier, while he was sitting here with me for our morning coffee, he pointed out an advertisement in this most established of newspapers and recommended that I pursue it. Now I am not a man easily shocked, but surely my mouth was agape at his suggestion! You

Wanted: Rich & handsome men to escort LADIES! LADIES! LADIES! Over 40,000 ladies want You! Now!

see, he, in front of my darling Turk's cap, handed me an advertisement for, how to say, prostitutes! Yes! With my innocent and pure Turk's cap standing directly aligned to see the paper, he put in before my eyes and boldly stated, Adam, my dear man, this is a calling for you! You have forty thousand women to choose from, and surely one of them could give you some physical pleasure, am I right?

I certainly don't need to state that my face turned more scarlet than a stop sign. Of course, my dear Turk's cap giggled girlishly and whispered, Herr Doktor, are you having some physical difficulties that only a woman can solve?

Oh the memory of that humiliation! I could hardly speak. I desired only to hide myself, but I do believe that I should be not embarrassed because I managed to carry myself with pride directly to the bathroom to cry and masturbate, in that order. As I ejaculated, and if truth is truth, I must confess that it was a magnificent orgasm, the type of orgasm that can only be attained when a person is in a pained emotional state, I came to understand that I must stop loving my darling Turk's cap.

You see, even I write this and even I sit here gazing adoringly at my Turk's cap, I understand that a man such as myself cannot have someone so lovely and wonderous as she is, and further more, I know that if a close friend of mine could humiliate me in such a hard manner, surely, she would do the same if only later in the future. You see, if truth is truth, I must confess that she is as arbitrary as anything else, as these photographs so beautiful in *The New York Times*, as the date of today, and if the news and these photographs could be changed and, how to say, manipulated in the manner in which I have manipulated them, then surely, my unwavering adoration for my darling Turk's cap can be changed until I find that I love her no longer.

I must confess, if truth is truth, that this will be difficult journey for me, being the modest man that I am, to forget about this love I have formed for my darling Turk's cap. I am

most accustomed to sitting to here in the New Buffalo Café
and watching her flutter around like a beautiful butterfly.
I love that only I have noticed the manner in which she,
while holding the coffee pots,
uses her index finger to
trace the lines of

her
hand.
She is quite
wonderful to
me, and I look

outside, and the day looks so very desolate without the prospect of loving my darling Turk's cap.

Still, if truth is truth, the sun is shining, and everything is blooming in the most beautiful manner imaginable. I suppose that today will be a good day after all, and my little Turk's cap will continue to bloom as long as the snow stays far away.

The Pythagoreans believed that 4 was inseparably connected with the first known order in the world. To them, it was 4 that caused the change from nature to civilization by arranging a confusing multiplicity of

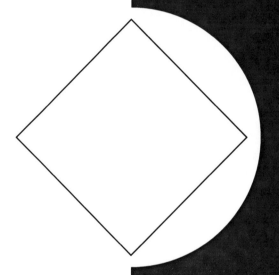

manifestations into various fixed forms. The first of these fixed forms was the solid. From 4 points emerge a solid object.

The Pythagoreans saw that 4 was the mathematical scheme created by nature.

chapter

4

CHICKEN

4

My feet sit on the floor, flat, not moving, cemented. I roll my fingers into two small balls bouncing on my knees that intersect the air with perfect perpendicular angles. I know what perpendicular angles are because Chi Hai taught me. She taught me that a perpendicular angle is the same thing as a right angle, and I asked her if there was a fancy word for a wrong angle. She told me to stop being smart, but I'm not really sure what that means and really, I only know that perpendicular and right are synonymous, but I don't really know what that means either. But still, I'm pretty sure that my knees are like perpendicular angles.

Squinting my face into something sour and holding as much air as my lungs can hold, I explode a grunt that sounds something between a sigh and a fart. I mean, it's pretty understandable because I've been pushing for over an hour. A whole hour. I know because I've been keeping time, and even though I know that Me Thu's clock is late because she always wants to be early, I know that if I'm timing myself, it doesn't really matter if the clock's late or early. I'm proud of myself for figuring that out, and even though I was pretty confused about it at first, I figured it out on my own. I also know that I've been pushing for an hour because my feet are asleep, tingling something fierce, like I'd been stepping on a million little fire ants all lined up in a row.

They always play tricks on me, and now my feet are sleeping and prickling like cacti, and it makes me mad because I don't always know they're tricks. They always pick on me, and I hate it, but then Chi Hai tells me that it's my job, which doesn't make sense to me because I don't get paid for it. She tells me that as the youngest, it's my responsibility to get picked on. I ask her what responsibility means, and she says that responsibility is duty, and I ask her what duty means, and she says that duty is something you can't run away from, like parents, and I say, But Chi Co ran away from my parents, and Chi Hai says, Be Ly, we don't talk about that. You know that, and all of a sudden, I'm worried that this whole chicken business is some sort of a joke.

So after I've been squatting here for an hour, I stand up and go find Chi Hai to tell here that I can't do it, that it isn't possible, that I can't be so easily tricked because I'm not stupid and I'm not a fool, and even though I'm the youngest, I'm not falling for any more tricks.

Be Ly, she says in the most condescending tone in the whole freaking world, you just weren't trying hard enough. The rest of us try to mimic the inflection of her voice when she does that, but no one else can find that perfect mixture of tenderness and disappointment. I know those words because Anh Son taught them to me. He told me that tender is the way our parents hug me when I do something smart, like memorizing a book and pretending that I could read it even though back then I was way too little to read, and disappointment is getting a B on my report card, and even though I'm not in school yet, I get what he means. I know how my parents can do that voice, but I still think that Chi Hai does it better.

In that tone, she says, Everyone knows that chickens can lay eggs, sweetheart, and you were born in the Year of the Chicken so you can lay eggs too. You have to believe me. I learned in it school, and when you start school, you'll start learning things like this too. Maybe you're just too little to do it, but I believe in you, sweetheart. Just go back there and try a little harder. I know you can.

Vietnamese families are titled differently than other families. We don't use names when referring to siblings. Instead, we label each person using a two-word system. The first word connotes gender and age relationship. An older brother is labeled, Anh, whereas and older sister is called, Chi. Ignoring gender, any younger sibling is thrown haplessly into the category, Em or Be, implying that the person with lesser years does not deserve a gender specific title, as if to say youth negates gendered expectations.

Of course, these expectations multiply as that young genderless child grows. If the older children fail their parents, all the expectation is transferred onto the shoulders of the young. It is a heavy burden. Translated, em means young and be means small. Put together, em be means baby.

So I go back into my corner in the kitchen. I hate it when she does that. I think Chi Hai is mean and that she shouldn't try to make me feel bad, and it isn't nice when people try to make other people cry or feel small, but there isn't any crying in Me Thu's house so I keep my tears in my eyes until they burn, and I have to rub my eyes because they burn so bad, but I don't let them out. I'm not a baby.

The second part of the name regards the order of birth. The oldest is given the number two, Hai; the second born the number three, Ba; the third the number four, Tu, and so on. A first-born girl, therefore, would be called Chi Hai by a younger sibling, and a second-born boy would be deemed Be Ba by the older sibling. We do not ever call each other by first names alone; it goes against tradition and shows grave disrespect.

The tile is cool against my bare feet as I start to resume squat position, slowly rocking my feet from sole to heel until my feet become rock flat against the tile. I love the tile floor at Me Thu's house. It's always crisp on my skin, unlike the floor at my house, which feels like there's this layer of ruddiness that can't go away until my mom, my real Me, can stay at home to take care of me and clean the floor on her hands and knees with a rag like Me Thu does, every day, usually twice a day. I mean, I know that she can't do it because my family needs that money and that even Me Thu is working even though she's at home, but sometimes, like right now, I don't want to have two families, two sets of parents and brothers and sisters. I don't need two sets of expectations for me now, and I really don't need to be taking care of two sets of parents when I grow up. Just thinking about it, I start to worry that I won't make enough money when I grow up because Me Thu says that she's simple but she's told me how she wants to retire and how I'll have to give her two hundred dollars month as payment for her taking care of me now, *just 200*, she says, but if I give that much to her, I'll have to give that much to Bo Hein too, and they're not even my real family so I'll have to give even more to my real Bo and Me, and the whole thing just makes my knees hurt like I've got arthritis, which Chi Hai says that I couldn't really have, that it's all in my head, because I'm only four, and how would a four-year-old have arthritis. It happens, I say. Sometimes, people aren't normal, like me, I'm not normal, so it makes sense that I could develop arthritis at a young age. Maybe if you were special too, you'd've had arthritis when you were four. I must've been pretty mad at her to tell her this, but I can't remember. I just remember getting put in time out for it.

It was a Wednesday. I'm sure it was a Wednesday, and I remember how opaque clouds lifted their skirts, and rain fell hard on my tangled mass of straight hair. I stood outside the elementary school waiting, wearing a pink skirt with tiny white bows. It was my favorite skirt. My t-shirt boasted blue and orange stripes. That morning, I'd carefully deliberated over which ensemble would look most professional. I must've tried on four or five different outfits. It wasn't everyday that my sister visited me at school to dash me away from a disappointing cafeteria lunch to have a meal at a real restaurant. Chi Co was fancy. She was my hero.

So I go back to my position on the floor, determined not to disappoint Chi Hai again. I hate it when I feel like a disappointment, a failure. When I watch tv, which isn't very often but I watch seven minutes of headline news with Bo before he goes to work at 7am Monday through Friday, and Wheel of Fortune and Jeopardy at 5 when he gets home from work, while Anh Son is cooking dinner, and I see other kids, I think that they're not like me, that they're outside playing, and sometimes, I wonder why I'm inside reading books, but I mean, I'm the youngest so I have to catch up to everyone else so I guess it makes sense that I have to work harder.

I can't believe I hadn't thought about that before! Of course, I have to work harder. If I want to lay eggs like a chicken, I have to think like a chicken, and I have to become like a chicken. Chi Hai told me a couple of weeks ago that chickens are birds because they have wings but they aren't really like birds because they can't fly. Penguins are also like that. I like penguins. They're fat and floppy. But anyways, the biggest difference between chickens and me is that I don't have wings. So I contort my body as if I were a chicken walking through the kitchen, pretending that my elbows were wings. And I think about what it would be like to have wings that were useless, constantly in the way but doing nothing. I think about what it would be like if my arms didn't really do anything, if they just hung there, but that isn't really the equivalent to a chicken because chickens can move their wings so I pretend that I can move my arms but I can't do anything else but move them. I think about how Chi Hai can get that mean look in her face and I start to flap my elbows about, pretending I was a chicken preparing to take flight, fully knowing that I can't fly, but if I'm a chicken, I don't have the brain power to distinguish stuff like that, and so I really become a chicken, flapping all crazy and pushing that egg out as hard as I can, pushing so hard that I choke on little bits of spit that get caught in my throat from trying to hold my breath for too long. I used to do that a lot though so it wasn't a big deal.

I don't call my real older sister Chi Hai or my real older brother Anh Ba. My parents didn't have the luxury of spending days with me. Instead, I stayed over at a family friend's home. As such, I had two families. My own parents, who I called Me, mother, and Bo, father, and my second parents, Me Thu, literally translated as Mother Fall, and Bo Hein, Gentle Father. I called my second parents' children by the proper Vietnamese sibling titles. I distinguished my own siblings by using their first names. I called my sister, Chi Co, and my brother, Anh Son.

I even start squawking like a chicken. And I'm squawking and pushing and flapping and even trying to let my elbows raise me off the ground, and just like that, I'm not doing any of those things any more because I'm not really sure how, but suddenly, I'm just a jumbled mass twisted into something real weird in the middle of the kitchen. I feel a big bump on my chin and again, I close my eyes hard to stop myself from crying until it burns a lot and I open my eyes and I'm not crying but I'm really close when Anh Ba and Chi Tu rush in to laugh at me. They even point their fingers that look like chicken legs at me. When Chi Hai arrives, I can't hold it back any more and I whimper that I can't do it, that I can't lay an egg, that I tried to be a chicken and it didn't work and now I'm actually crying real fat tears, and I don't want to be a chicken any more. Anh Ba's laughter slows into thick snorts.

In Vietnamese tradition, the children take care of the parents when they get old. This is the third world equivalent to Social Security. When my families came to the States, they assumed that their children would take care of them when they got older, that their tradition would be our tradition.

Chi Hai says, Be Ly, look at Be Tu. She was born in the Year of the Dragon, and you know what she can do?

What? I say. What can Chi Tu do?

I think to myself, You're not stupid. You're not going to fall for any quick tricks.

She can breathe fire, she says.

She cannot, I say.

She has be really really mad, she says.

She cannot, I say.

I mean really mad, she says.

She cannot, I say.

If you don't believe me, why don't you go stomp on her toes? You know how much she hates that, she says.

She cannot, I say.

Be Ly, if you don't believe me, I dare you, she says.

She cannot, I say.

Try it then, smarty-pants, she says.

Fine!, I'm really mad. I can't believe she thinks I'm so stupid that I'm going to fall for this trick. I mean, who's dumb enough to go stomp on Chi Tu's feet? She was born in the Year of the Dragon, and you can tell because she had the worst temper out of all of us. I was afraid of her, and I didn't need her to breathe fire to tell me that.

> My mom had forgotten to give me an umbrella that morning. She often forgot practical things like that.

But I wanted to see if she really could breathe fire. So I start running towards Chi Tu, as fast as I can, which isn't really that fast because I have arthritis, and about a yard before I reach her, I prepare to jump, like the people in the Olympics that jump across the big sand pit, and I take off and I swear I'm in the air for at least five seconds, and I land right on her toes.

Be Ly!, she yells. What'd you think you're doing? What'd you do that, you little brat?

I don't say anything and sprint like I don't have arthritis to hide behind Chi Hai's legs. I take my hands to cover my eyes, but really, I peek through the slats of fingers so I can see because I really want to see, and I see Chi Tu reach her arms backwards, so far back that it looks like they're not even connected to her body any more, and her head leans forward until she's as long as a real dragon. And then, she does it. For a second, I can't believe it, but it's real. With lips molded into an open O the size of a coffee mug, she blows fire right on top of the stove top. It was a big fire too, much bigger than the stove can ever make. So it's true. Chi Hai wasn't lying to me. We all have special powers from our zodiac signs.

Now do you believe me?, Chi Hai says.

I nod my head, still hiding behind her pants so she can't see me.

Even today, I don't have the nerve to disrespect any of my siblings, real or otherwise, by calling them by their American names. I avoid having to address them because I don't want to speak Vietnamese in public, like it's a mark of shame. But they've all adjusted. They call each other by their American names. Maybe it's just because they're older or maybe I've been trained so well that I can't break the only tradition I know.

So I squat again, in the kitchen, for two hours. I watch the electric clock on the stove change minutes. I'm counting because I want to keep track of how long it'll take me lay an egg because I want to be practical about this. I mean, if it only takes me a few hours of squatting to lay an egg then I could lay enough eggs to feed my family by squatting for a whole day. If I could do that, then Me wouldn't have to work so much. I could help her workload, and besides, my family likes eating fried eggs. I squash my eyes shut and grunt like the woman having a baby, I know about that because I saw a movie with a woman having a baby and it looked like it hurt, but I'd been in this kitchen for hours thinking like a chicken so neither situation could be that much worse than the other. And so like that woman having a baby, I push because that's what the doctor and her husband told the pregnant woman to do. I can feel it coming, almost like I was taking a poop but not really. And then, almost like nothing had really changed at all, I feel something underneath my butt.

I open my eyes and there's this little speckled egg right below my butt. I laid an egg! I made this egg real. I laid an egg.

I run to find Chi Hai. She looks at the egg, takes it from my hands, and inspects it.

She says, Be Ly, this is a tiny egg. Can't you do any better than that?

I say, But it's a real egg. Look. I laid an egg.

She says, But it's so small. I bet you can't even eat this egg it's so small.

Contemplating, I say, But it's just because I'm little too. I can only lay little egg rights now. When I get bigger, will I be able to lay bigger eggs?

No, Be Ly. I think this is all you can you. It's pretty disappointing, she says.

By the time school administrators with serious pants and cement faces came outside, my overstuffed backpack was drenched. My eyes were disappointment. I tried to explain that Chi Co was coming to pick me up, that she promised me on Monday that she would come on Wednesday because I hated Wednesdays because it was Mexican food day, that she told me she would be here and I was going to wait here until she got here because she promised. Jumbled words came out instead. I smashed my eyes together, making myself not cry in front on the principal. When I opened my eyes, it was still raining.

I run around the house, interrogating people to find out their sign. Anh Son was born twelve years before me so he was a chicken too. I make him squat down.

Be Ly, he says, Don't be so stupid! Boy chickens don't lay eggs. Only girl chickens do.

I think about it. Anh Son is a lot smarter than me. He's right. No boys lay eggs.

Chi Co drove a shiny red Jeep. Most days, the top was peeled off like an orange peel, but today, the canvas covering would be re-applied because it was raining. My eyes searched every road; I was unsure which route Chi Co would take.

Feeling stupid, I run up to Anh Ba, even though he's always the meanest to me, but I don't care because I just laid an egg and everyone should know about it. I run up to him and pull at the edge of his cotton shirt. It smelled like clean.

Anh Ba, I say, what year were you born in? What's your sign? What's your special power because I can lay eggs and I tried so hard all morning but I did it. I didn't think that I could, but I did.

Be Ly, he says, don't be stupid.

Smartly, I say, But it's true. We all have little special things that we can. Chi Tu can blow fire out of her mouth when she gets mad, remember? You were there. I can lay eggs, but they're really tiny, but they're still eggs.

She'd called on Monday. Chi Co had called me at home. She said that she missed me, that she would come pick me up any day that I want from school and we'd go have lunch. I didn't even hesitate. I told her Wednesday, and I was so excited because she promised. She promised.

My fingers uncoil a grayish egg. Anh Ba smiles at me like I'm a fool.

I hated Mexican food day. I hated Mexican food. As I shoved a spork full of cheese enchiladas in my mouth, I hated my sister, my only sister, my big sister. I didn't even chew the food. I could feel the clumps of greasy cheese struggle through my throat. I would never trust her again. She was a bad person. She left me at home, and she went away, and she couldn't even remember to come pick me up from school like she promised. She was liar, a cheat, and a bad person. I felt sick. Coughing lightly, I threw up everything on my favorite skirt.

That night, when I return to my home, my feet drag along the floor, trying to collect as much dirt as possible. I show my parents the egg.

I say, I made this. Are you proud? They kiss me on the forehead and tell me to go to bed.

> Although I can't bring myself to call anyone in my family by their American name, I also can't bear the idea of supporting my parents and their dreams that I'm bound to disappoint for the rest of my life.

I go to my room, close the door, and get ready for bed. I take off my shirt and unbutton my pants. I say, I hate you all so much. And this time, I clasp my eyes harder than I have all day and when I open my eyes, I haven't cried, but I'm closer than I've ever been because I was wearing pants, and chickens can't lay eggs through pants.

3 is the first number to create a geometrical figure.

Although the Pythagoreans wanted to see the world in patterns of 4, the variations on 3 were overwhelming. They saw 3 worlds: earth, water, & air; they saw three states: solid,

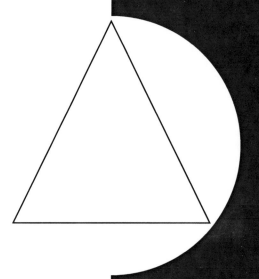

liquid, & gas; they saw 3 groups of created things: animal, plant, & mineral; and they saw three primary colors: red, yellow, & blue. They saw a world developed through triads.

They also used 3 to represent man, also, therefore, good.

chapter

3

DIVISION

There is a woman. She is beautiful.
Her eyes are velvet; her hair is breeze.
Her lips could grow a garden full
of the most exotic flowers, but they
wouldn't, unless forced. Her legs are
forests; her arms are the sky.

And still, she is sad.

Possessing all the beauty the earth
could offer, she cries. Often and
hard.
    Some say that rain is God
crying. Some say that her tears are
worth more than God's.
    But this is not about God. This
is about her. And she is still sad.

And the thorns shall come up in her palaces,
Nettles & brambles in the fortresses thereof;
And it shall be an habitation for jackals,
And a court for owls.
The wild wolves of the desert shall also meet with hyenas,
And the Sa'ir shall cry to his fellow;
Lilith also shall rest there,
And find for herself a place of rest.

— from THE BOOK OF ISAIAH

A. B. Adams, M.D., Ph.D
Psychiatrist, Psychologist, Psychotherapist
12 Babylon Dr., #3
South, IN 61221
(219) 354 - 0741

PART I: GENERAL PATIENT INFORMATION

Patient Name: _____
　　　　　　　　　(First)　　　　　(MI)　　　　　(Last)

Date of Birth: _____ / _____ / _____　　Age: _____

Address: _____
　　　　　　　　　(Street)

_____
　　(City)　　　　　　　　(State)　　　　　(Zip)

Current Medical Condition: _____

_____

_____

Primary Care Physician: _____

Prior Therapist(s): _____

Place of Employment: _____

Title/Position: _____

Level of Education: _____

Emergency Contact: _____

Home Phone: (_____) _____ - _____

Relationship to Patient: _____

Work Phone: (_____) _____ - _____

Referred to this Office by: _____

Once upon a time, there was a man sleeping in his house. The man who was sleeping was not a prince, although at that very moment, he was dreaming. In his dream, he was a knight with gold hair peaking between bits of iridescent armor. He rode a horse. The horse was black and wild, and he knew that only he could control this beast by gently touching him. Even though he was a knight, this man sleeping in his house didn't know why he was a knight. Even in his dreams, he lacked ambition.

Rather than save a beautiful princess or challenge another knight to a joust or find the Holy Grail, he wandered around with his horse. Mostly, he rode the horse; other times, he would get off and walk it, but the horse loved his touch so much that when the knight's body was displaced from his own, he would rise up on two hooves and yelp whinnies until the man sleeping in his house who was dreaming he was a knight returned to his proper position on his horse's back. The horse had lovely green eyes. Eyes that looked almost human. Eyes that could be loving.

And so the knight continued to travel with the horse, never getting off his back, never wanting the horse to be upset, and in his dreams, he wanders and wanders and wanders, and the man sleeping in his house started **ONE** to believe that he really was a knight because this dream lasted so long. He had to admit that he didn't mind being a knight either. In fact, as the dream drew itself, he began to love the horse. He changed her gender, gently caressed her velvet skin, toyed with naming her. At night, he would lie on her back, feel her breath change under him, masturbate, cum in her mane, and kiss himself to sleep knowing that he was unworthy of her.

In his dream that night after masturbating, she transformed into the most beautiful woman, with a horse's mane of thick black hair. She was so perfect he couldn't touch her. This beautiful woman called to him. She slipped her hands over her body. There were no imperfections. This man dreaming in his house, he knew that he couldn't have her. He knew that even when she was a horse, their love was wrong, but now that she was human flesh, he couldn't. He just couldn't, even though his penis was so erect he could barely walk. He couldn't explain why he felt this way, but he did know that her beauty tipped the scale of equality so far that he couldn't imagine an existence without her. And in his dream, he cut her thick mane and made a noose, and he did not wake up.

It is impossible to say that Lilith seduced this man to death. It is only known that he died mid-dream.

PART II: INSURANCE INFORMATION

Primary Insurance Company: _____

Phone: (_____) _____ - _____

Address: _____
                (Street)

_____
   (City)   (State)   (Zip)

Name of Policy Holder: _____

Relationship to Patient: _____

Policy Number: _____

Secondary Insurance Company: _____

Street Address: _____
                     (Street)

_____
   (City)   (State)   (Zip)

Phone: (_____) _____ - _____

Name of Policy Holder: _____

Relationship to Patient: _____

Policy Number: _____

INSURANCE AUTHORIZATION

I hereby authorize DR. ADAMS to furnish any information to my carrier(s) concerning my illness and treatments.

_____   _____
    (Signature)   (Date)

If a body were divided into three parts,
would they be equal?

Made from dirt and dust, not from the same fresh soil, she is not his equal, but she refuses to lie below him. She refuses to be his slave. She speaks the name of God and is erased from the memory of all, but she was there first. Before woman, there was Lilith.		

Lilith adorns herself with all kinds of decorations, like
an amorous woman. She stands at the entrance to roads
and paths, in order to seduce men. She seizes the fool
who approaches her, kisses him and fills him with wine
whose dregs contain snake venom. As soon as he has
drunk this, he starts to follow her.

— from ZOHAR

PART III: PATIENT HISTORY

Have you or any member of your family had:

ILLNESS	YOURSELF		YOUR FAMILY	
	Yes	No	Yes	No
High Blood Pressure	☐	☐	☐	☐
Thyroid or Metabolism Trouble	☐	☐	☐	☐
Diabetes	☐	☐	☐	☐
Kidney/Bladder Trouble	☐	☐	☐	☐
Stroke or Heart Attack	☐	☐	☐	☐
Convulsions	☐	☐	☐	☐
Ulcers	☐	☐	☐	☐
Liver Problems	☐	☐	☐	☐
Electroshock Treatment	☐	☐	☐	☐
Drug or Alcohol Problems	☐	☐	☐	☐
Phobias	☐	☐	☐	☐
Problems with the Police	☐	☐	☐	☐
Depression	☐	☐	☐	☐
Anxiety	☐	☐	☐	☐
Suicidal Attempts or Thoughts	☐	☐	☐	☐
Other Mental Diseases	☐	☐	☐	☐

PART IV: FAMILY HISTORY

FATHER:
Living ☐   Deceased ☐   Age: _____

MOTHER:
Living ☐   Deceased ☐   Age: _____

BROTHER(S):
Living ☐   Deceased ☐   Age: _____

SISTER(S):
Living ☐   Deceased ☐   Age: _____

Please list all SEVERE ILLNESSES you have experienced and/or any OPERATIONS you have undergone:

SEVERE ILLNESSES	Age	OPERATIONS	Age
_____	_____	_____	_____
_____	_____	_____	_____
_____	_____	_____	_____
_____	_____	_____	_____
_____	_____	_____	_____
_____	_____	_____	_____
_____	_____	_____	_____

Please list all names of MEDICATIONS with the name of the PHYSICIAN:

MEDICATION	PHYSICIAN
_____	_____
_____	_____
_____	_____
_____	_____
_____	_____
_____	_____
_____	_____

Once upon a time, in a city, much like any other city, there is a woman. The woman is not a princess or even royalty, but she is a mother, and not just any mother, but a new mother. She has just given birth to a beautiful baby girl. She hasn't even had time to pick out a name yet.

This new mother's face is shiny with sweat, but it isn't like the movies or television. She isn't radiant or beautiful. Instead, the sweat sticks to her face like grease, and not fresh grease but grease that's been used to fry a couple vats of bacon for a restaurant. Her face is an ugly brown grease trap, but still, her baby looks at her admiringly.

Now this woman, she's always considered herself to be a brave person. She's not one to shy away from pain. In fact, she just had her baby without any anesthetic, and she feels great, but then, she looks at her baby, and suddenly, things don't feel so right anymore. It's like the movies, the way a soft shadow drapes over her bed to show that something's about to go very wrong. The shadow grows so large that it seems to drink the entire room. She looks up from her baby and sees a woman.

The woman has wild black hair looping snakes still slithering. Her face is perfection, and she wears black as though black is her skin and not her clothing. She smiles bright red and a silk hand reaches over and removes the baby from her arms.

The new mother doesn't know what to do. She watches as her baby is tucked neatly under this woman's arm, beneath three other babies and on top of two more babies. She holds a sack filled with sleeping infants, each one wrinkled red, barely even smooth. The new mother looks in and she can count at least thirty babies, and for the first time since this woman walked into her room, she's scared. She wants to scream but doesn't. Frantically, she looks around the room for the emergency button, but it's too far away to reach.

While the new mother panics, the woman in black rearranges the babies, tossing them into the air, and each one floats down into her bag, barely breaking the silence of frenzy. Down the line of the maternity ward, each new mother wears the same look as this new mother, almost as though they were wearing the same mask.

There is no way to prove that Lilith stole this woman's baby. It is only known that thirty-three babies disappeared from one hospital on the same day. It was the largest baby theft recorded in that small town.

PART V: RELATIONSHIP HISTORY

MARITAL STATUS:
Single ☐　　　Married ☐　　　Divorced ☐　　　Widowed ☐

Length of current marriage: _____

Number of previous marriages: _____

Spouse's Name: _____

Children's Name(s)　　　　　　　　Age(s)

_____　　_____

_____　　_____

_____　　_____

_____　　_____

_____　　_____

Miscarriages:　　☐　Yes　　☐　No

If yes, please describe the experience: _____

_____

_____

_____

_____

_____

_____

Any additional comments regarding Family or Marital History: _____

_____

_____

_____

_____

_____

_____

PART VI: RELATIONSHIPS & EMOTIONS

Please list adjectives describing your PARENTS or how your parents make you feel. For instance: warm, loving, cold, distant, angry, passive, aggressive, sad.

FATHER   MOTHER

_____   _____

_____   _____

_____   _____

_____   _____

_____   _____

_____   _____

_____   _____

_____   _____

_____   _____

Please adjectives describing YOURSELF and your SPOUSE or PARTNER (if applicable).

SELF   SPOUSE/PARTNER

_____   _____

_____   _____

_____   _____

_____   _____

_____   _____

_____   _____

_____   _____

_____   _____

_____   _____

If a body were divided into three parts,
would they be equal?

| | | To prostitutes, she is a goddess. She is their leader. A sexual provocateur with hypnotic eyes, men cannot restrain desires with her. She revels in destroying marriage and love, anything sacred. She is the enemy of every woman but the whore. |
| | | |

In the name of the great God, Amen. Hallelujah, for
ever, Amen. Peace for Marian, daughter of S., and the
unborn child of her womb, from the Lilith of her bridal
bed.

— from a Palenstinian amulet

Once upon a time, archeologists found old artifacts in Southern Babylonia. The artifacts were a series of bowls, buried, with lips tightly kissing to deny any speck of dirt entrance. All around the digging grounds were these bowls, always clamped shut, all intricately painted and designed. Inside each bowl was an inscription.

Once upon a time, archeologists combined forces with cultural anthropologists and theologians and linguists and scientists to rebuild a story to accompany these now unburied bowls. Sitting in museums, naked and halved through excavations, these bowls carry a story with them that all the archeologists and anthropologists and theologians and linguists and scientists never thought of.

The experts' story went like this:

Once upon a time, there was a demon that was floating around, torturing and tormenting people, especially handsome men and new mothers. One day, the village priest came up with the solution. He combined forces with the village artisans, and together, they molded bowls. Each bowl was unique and given the utmost care by the most skillful potters and artists. Inside the bowls were written an **THREE** incantation against the demon. The idea was that the moment the demon tried to harm a villager by entering his or her body, he or she would drink from this bowl and the demon would be caught as the incantation was read out loud. After all the liquid was drained and the demon was trapped, another bowl would seal the demon inside. The demon cage would be buried for safekeeping. The number of burials in the area shows how superstitious and fearful these villagers were.

The experts' story, however, has many holes. The bowls carry the true story. If the bowls had a voice, they would mock the experts and ask them the most elementary questions that they would have no answer for. The bowls, by questioning, would reveal the in-expertise of these experts. They would ask them why a demon would want to enter someone's body. They would ask how someone could say an incantation while drinking water. They would interrogate the experts as to how drinking, a consumptive act, would remove a demon from the body, a creative act. The bowls would ask what demon it was, but of course, the bowls wouldn't need to ask. They would already know the answers.

If the bowls could speak, they would tell the experts how wrong their story was. They would tell them that the bowls were not used for drinking at all. Rather, they were placed outside homes and filled with fresh sacrificial blood. The demons passing would not be able to resist such a delicacy. When they (the demons) drank from the bowls, they would be imprisoned because of the curse written on the interior. The villagers, seeing the blood drained, would clasp another bowl on top of the original and bury them in front of their main door for eternal protection. The bowls would tell those so-called experts that the villagers weren't that superstitious. There were so many bowls because of two coincidences. The first was that there were many animals that nourished themselves with blood, which is to say that it was not necessarily a demon that drained the blood, although the villagers did not realize this. The second coincidence was that there was indeed a demon that tortured and tormented the villagers, and she did like fresh blood, although she never drank it.

PART VII: STRESS AND NERVOUS SYSTEM QUESTIONNAIRE

Please answer to the best of your ability.

Do you experience stress frequently? ☐ Yes ☐ No

Do you have palpitations or irregular heartbeat? ☐ Yes ☐ No

Do you sometimes have difficulty breathing? ☐ Yes ☐ No

Do you sweat unusually? ☐ Yes ☐ No

Do you feel stress or tension while working? ☐ Yes ☐ No

Are you often nervous or tense? ☐ Yes ☐ No

Do you lose your temper frequently? ☐ Yes ☐ No

Do you get upset easily? ☐ Yes ☐ No

Do you feel that you worry too much? ☐ Yes ☐ No

Do you worry about physical illness? ☐ Yes ☐ No

Do you experience unusual forgetfulness? ☐ Yes ☐ No

Have you ever had a severe head injury? ☐ Yes ☐ No

Have you ever experienced seizures or epilepsy? ☐ Yes ☐ No

Have you ever been delirious or unconscious? ☐ Yes ☐ No

How make cups of coffee to you drink in a day? _____

Do you smoke? ☐ Yes ☐ No

For how many years? _____ Number per day _____

How much alcohol do you consume per day? _____ week? _____

What do you do for relaxation? _____

_____

_____

*If a body were divided into three parts,
would they be equal?*

When she spoke the name of God, he cursed her to the life of a demon. She had to strip babies of their mothers before their 20th day alive. This was not the loving, altruistic God of the New Testament. If she did not steal babies, 10,000 of her own would die for every one that she allowed to live.

*You must never again appear in his house, nor in her
room, nor in her bedchamber. For you should you,
Lilith, whose father is Palhas and whose mother is
Pelahdad, that R. Josua ben Perachja has proclaimed a
ban against you. I conjure you by Palhas, your father,
and Pelahdad, your mother: A divorce certificate
has come to us from heaven. In this is written some
formation and warning for you, for you, in the name of
Palsa-Pelisha. You, Lilith, male Lili and female Lilith,
shelanitha and chatiphata, you are banished… I tear
out the evil stranglers and their evil Liliths. Do not ever
return to them from this day forward. Amen.*

— from an Aramaic incantation bowl

Once upon a time, God created Adam with one hand. In that hand, he held dirt and clay that was not brown. It was clean and pure. In the other hand, he held dirt and clay that was really dirt and clay. With that hand, he made Lilith.

Once upon a time, Adam and Lilith lived together in Eden. They seemed to be a happy couple. She picked berries while he folded leaves into a quilt. While she was busy developing various modes of agriculture, he wandered around Eden finding different ways to decorate the quilt, which by now had grown to be the size of a mattress. He gathered rose petals and weaved them together with kisses to place beneath Lilith's head. He knew his wife was quite amazing, but she was always working, doing new things. She invented a till to make gardening easier. She dug a canal to more efficiently irrigate her crops. During the cold nights, she rubbed sticks to make warmth, and afterwards, she held Adam close.

Their relationship was more than ideal, especially for Adam, except for one slight problem. When they fornicated, and they did indeed fornicate, especially with the bed Adam wove, Lilith didn't

ONE (ONCE AGAIN)

want to be on the bottom. Her husband may not have believed in much, but he believed that the man should be on top, and he believed it staunchly. Lilith was unable to compromise on this topic, and obviously, neither was Adam.

Every time after Adam climaxed, Lilith would leave the bed and go work in the garden. She sighed angrily but continued to bring home food for her husband, who continued to build furniture out of leaves. He made plates out of lily pads and silverware out of dried weeds, and she brought home more and more exotic plants to consume. No matter how satiated Adam became, he still would not let her be on top. Years passed. Finally frustrated with her forced sexual obeisance, she spoke the name of God and was whisked away from Eden.

And neither Adam nor Lilith lived happily ever after. But then again, neither did Eve.

PART VIII: OUTLOOK, THOUGHT, AND MOOD QUESTIONNAIRE

I often have trouble concentrating.	☐ Yes	☐ No
People often talk about me behind my back.	☐ Yes	☐ No
I am often jealous.	☐ Yes	☐ No
It's hard for me to focus my attention.	☐ Yes	☐ No
I see and hear things that others don't.	☐ Yes	☐ No
I often feel depressed or despondent.	☐ Yes	☐ No
My enthusiasm is decreased.	☐ Yes	☐ No
I have trouble sleeping (too much or too little).	☐ Yes	☐ No
I have abnormal sexual interest (too much or little).	☐ Yes	☐ No
I get dizzy or light-headed.	☐ Yes	☐ No
I feel guilty often.	☐ Yes	☐ No
My mood varies from day to night.	☐ Yes	☐ No
I have lost the ability to have fun.	☐ Yes	☐ No
I have low self-esteem.	☐ Yes	☐ No
I have lost strength and energy.	☐ Yes	☐ No
I tend to bottle up my feelings.	☐ Yes	☐ No
It is hard for me express anger or resentment.	☐ Yes	☐ No
I have been sexually abused.	☐ Yes	☐ No
I find it necessary to juggle sexual partners.	☐ Yes	☐ No
I have experimented with homosexuality.	☐ Yes	☐ No
I have gained or lost at least 5 pounds recently.	☐ Yes	☐ No
I often have headaches.	☐ Yes	☐ No

PART IX: MATCHING

Please match each word with its closet corresponding characteristic.
You may not use any trait twice.

Mother	Past
Smart	Forgot
Period	Expectation
Division	Molestation
Separation	Pain
Memory	Future
Smoke	Weight
Laughter	Fear
Depression	Sex
Change	Home
Family	Sickness
Father	Prayer

If a body were divided into three parts, it could be equal, but this is not the story of a body divided into three parts. This is a story about a woman divided into much more than three small parts, much more than three different personalities.

If Lilith were a person, she would be insane. She would be caught between wanting too many things, with too many expectations unfulfilled. She is not a superhuman. She cannot be ideal and flawed, mother and whore, killer and victim. She has become an empty form for people to fill with their own ideas. To feminists, she is a hero. To some, she was the first woman. To others, she is a demon. To most, she does not exist and has never existed. This much is certain though: if Lilith were a human, she would have

The day Li[...] Eden she w[...] and scared [...] missed her [...] his calming [...] She looked [...]

When she [...] the name of [...]

Made from dirt and dust, not from the [...]

To pro[...]

Every woman wanted to be her. Despite he[...] status as a demon [...] here was somethin[...] ure and lovely abou[...] r that no one den[...] rhaps it was jus[...] cause she [...] e first. Perha[...] as her beauty [...] apped men [...] ade women en[...] ith rage.

And her children hungry children gnawed on her flesh from her insides until their teeth made [...]

And Lilith slithered up to Eve and said, Eat it, my darling. Why would God have a tree filled with fruit if he did not want you to eat it? She smiled the way only a serpent could and slithered into the reflecting pool. Eve, sitting there hungry, reached up into the tree.

When she spoke the name of God, he cursed to forever live in a mirror, looking out at the world that she [...] o leave looking iful and ilith was demon rror her

The day Lilith left Eden she was cold and scared. She missed her husband, his calming touches. She looked up to God and begged him to allow her back into Eden. She said, God, I beg you. I submit to you, and He didn't

forgiveness, and God, in his rage, looked on her and watched her suffer while smiling broadly.

She is the enemy of

And Lilith slithered up to Eve and said, Eat it, my darling. Why would God have a tree filled with fruit if he did not want you to eat it? She smiled the way only a serpent could and slithered into the reflecting pool. Eve, sitting there hungry, reached up into the tree.

When she spoke the name of God, he cursed to forever live in a mirror, looking out at the world that she was forced to leave behind, always looking at Eve, beautiful and untouchable. Lilith was known as the demon of vanity. A mirror her eternal prison.

And her children hungry children gnawed on her flesh from her insides until their teeth made

Every woman wanted to be her. Despite her status as a demon there was something ure and lovely abou r that no one deny erhaps it was jus ecause she e first. Perha as her beauty apped men ade women en ith rage.

Made from dirt and dust, not from the

The day Li Eden she w and scared missed her his calming She looked

forgiveness, and God, in his rage, looked on her and watched her suffer while smiling broadly.

PART X: CONTRACTS & SIGNATURES

I, _____, verify that all of the information submitted about is true and answered to the best of my capabilities.

_____   _____
(Signature)   (Date)

_____
(Printed Name)

I understand that all information I have provided and my therapy sessions are completely confidential; however, Dr. Adams and his associates are allowed to discuss overall treatment plans, diagnoses, and medications prescribed to insurance companies, for anonymous psychiatric studies, and for legal reasons. I, _____, hereby allow Dr. Adams and his associates to release my medical information for the aforementioned purposes and understand the full ramifications of this contract.

_____   _____
(Signature)   (Date)

_____
(Printed Name)

When the Almighty—may his name be praised—
created the first, solitary man, He said: It is not good
for man to be alone. And He fashioned for man a
woman from the earth, like him (Adam), and called her
Lilith. Soon, they began to quarrel with each other. She
said to him: I will not lie underneath, and he said: I
will not lie underneath but above, for you are meant to
lie underneath and I to lie above. She said to him: We
are both equal, because we are both (created) from the
earth. But they didn't listen to each other. When Lilith
saw this, she pronounced God's avowed name and flew
into the air.

— from ALPHABET OF BEN SIRA

There is a woman sitting in the waiting room of an office. She is beautiful. Her eyes are crushed velvet; her hair is misting breeze. Her lips could grow a garden full of the most fragrant flowers but they wouldn't, unless forced. Her legs are deforested; her arms are thunderbolts.

And still, she is.

Possessing all the beauty the earth could offer, she cries. Often and hard.
Some say that rain is God crying. Some say that her tears are worth more than God's.
But this is not about God. This is about her. And she is still sad.

Her name is Lilith.

*The line, the geometric expression of 2,
separates as it unites.*

——————————

*To the Pythagoreans, 2 was contradiction
and antithesis.*

*2 also symbolizes Eve, the second human,
the fall of man.*

chapter

2

intersections

INSTRUCTIONS: Find 78 words.

```
A T L A S A D I S T H T I L I L
R R N H O N K N U D O M I N A N
G R E N S P E C I E S T R O K E
O E B Y P L A U M Q E I I V Y E
C L T O T E I L S M O U F N N I
S O O R H R L A E S A L A F E R
A U H L F A I Y P M R I S E D E
N C F L G O D I O B E V O S R C
E Y O S H E X P E C T A T I O N
G S U O R T X E D I M A Z H A T
D R E A M T G I N G I V I T I S
A A M A N T E I V P H Y S I C S
P R E E N D A I N D I C A T O R
A I R A S T R O N O M E R C S L
B G L M T O E U T U R K S C A P
S O Y R T C C Y L F R E T T U B
M L T N G D E L T A C M A D A U
R A A M E R I C A N O G A R D O
O N S R I T A U Q E R E H E V E
S E H E I Q B O O A H C G E N I
S U E N N I L K P L A C E K O M
X E V E O D B C E L L B A M Y D
```

The Pythagoreans did not consider 1 a real number. A number, they reasoned, was an aggregate made up of various units. Nothing

but 1 makes up 1. They believed that 1 was not a number but a producer, a mother, the foundation for all other numbers.

chapter

I

: WEIGHT

I

I watch him struggling. A permanent layer of sweat causes the weight to slide from his ruddy shoulders down to his upper back. I hear a firm crack that sounds more like skin breaking than bone popping. His face is leathered and slick, and it convulses every couple of seconds. I know his burden is too great to afford flaws like that.

He isn't what I expected. Truthfully, I'm a little disappointed. When I thought of him, I thought of all the pictures I'd seen. He's most often depicted with a perfect bronze tan, a tan attainable from either superficial light or a lifetime under the sun; his hair color fluctuates between blonde or brown flowing locks, but always, in every portrayal I've seen, he's got blue eyes. Usually, he wears some hybrid of loincloth and toga, something provocative but undeniably masculine. In the pictures, his weight is the earth, large and untamable.

The man before me though, he's a real man. His hair and eyes are the color of sorrow, whichever shade of sadness he feels that day, sometimes it's a storm grey, sometimes it's deep shadow. His skin is adobe and just as strong. Surprisingly, he wears clothes like a regular man, but really, the most important thing about him, the part that everyone cares most about, is his weight, the punishment that he must carry on his shoulders. I've read many versions of his story. Some say that his burden is the world; others say it is the heavens, but neither is accurate. His weight is the weight of expectation, and it's a huge mass of lead denser than lead.

His feet shuffle methodically. I watch him try to lift his thick soles fully off the red sand, but he can only muster enough strength to drag them across dirt so coarse it can cut even the most calloused skin. The bottoms of his feet are crusted with mud.

His face remains still, other than the brief convulsions of pain. I wish he would smile. It would make my spying more comfortable.

When our silence creates a low annoying buzz, he speaks, slowly, with deliberation. His voice is a hum, but it cracks of solitude.

He asks, Why are you here?

I laugh because he is great, he is a legend, and he has asked me a human question, more than a human question. He has just asked me an obvious question. I laugh at his simplicity. I laugh because I can't compile adequate words to respond.

With my laughter, he inches his feet to turn himself around. He is a child that doesn't get his way, a child threatening to leave but not really wanting to go yet. I am a fool, and I fall for his juvenile psychological tricks.

I say, I want to help with your burden. I want to transfer some of the weight from your shoulders to mine.

He says, Go.

He says, Leave me alone.

His voice is gentle, singing a requiem, perhaps his own requiem, perhaps someone else's, like Mozart, like so many others. There is a softness about him, a resigned sadness. I know he doesn't trust me. I wonder if he can trust anyone.

He says, How did you find me?

His skin crackles, I imagine that inside him, his bones are shedding their outer sheathes. I imagine shards of calcium forcing the expansions of his arteries, making his blood elastic.

It's beautiful here, a version of Eden without shades of green. Everything around him is a different variation of red, even the rocks. I wonder which came first, him or his environment. He is a chameleon. Behind him, large burnt sienna boulders are hardly decipherable against the blood sky.

I say, As a girl, I read your stories. Now that I am a woman and must trade my time for money, I study maps. I search for things hidden. I came here to find dragons. After I saw them, I ventured further, and then I found you, here, wilting under a pressure unknown to any other human.

He says, There are no dragons here. You're a liar.

I say, If I didn't see dragons, how can I see you?

He says, You're a liar! Why must you lie to me? There aren't any dragons here!

I laugh because he is angry. I laugh because he is antiquated.

I say, Then I don't know how I got here. I only know that I went looking for dragons, I found them, and now I've found you.

He nods his head, but it isn't a vertical nod. Rather, his head sways from side to side, heavy, the way I remember my father swaying his head. Sadly he says, Now that you've found me, I know more will come. I need a new home.

He looks as though I've smothered his world. His eyes change from gray to blue to the shadows of cacti without flowers. I watch, and each color is distinct and each color is dolor. Once, while I spoke, they flickered the color of dried lily petals, a strange beauty found only in death. Now, his eyes are the color of envy desiring.

Knowing that I've upset him, I excuse myself, but before I leave, I ask, May I return another time? It must be lonely here without any companionship or conversation.

He says, If you're not here to hurt me, to steal the punishment that is rightfully mine, you may come back, but please know, I'm not easily fooled. I've been fooled once before, and it won't happen again, but I must confess, I'm fond of your voice. It's delicate, and you've traveled far to reach here, and I must perform the role of host amiably.

Thanks, I say, not out of spite or facetiousness, but out of real thanks. I know this is something great. He is exactly how I imagined, beautiful and sad, and even though he looks nothing like I thought he would, he is exactly how I imagined. He stands here, before me, immortal and lovely, as he has stood for thousands of years.

As I walk away, all the little red pebbles shy away from my feet. I'm surprised to see below the superficial layer, the soil isn't even red. It's real soil. It's brown.

The plants turn away from the sunshine that bakes my hair crisp; they turn away from me. Pausing, I breathe in his world through my skin, but now, I notice even the red mountains begin to shun me. Their peaks point outward. It's noticeable. I wonder why this place is unhappy with me. I'm an intruder, I understand that, but I'm not trying to find myself a home here on the edge of the map, I'm just looking. I wonder if curiosity should be hated like this.

In my dimly furnished hotel room, I pull out the photographs that brought me here. I examine the intricate details of the 1503 Lenox globe. I study its nuances against waves of candlelight. This in an old place I stay in. It lacks electricity. It is antiquated, like him. Wax rolls to burn my pinky finger. I laugh because I've just now realized that the wax is red. I laugh because something red finally wants to be near me.

Exhausted from days of trying travel, I think of the way we create mythologies, how giants are made, and I consider the possibility that all heroes were once just men and women and slowly they emerged something new from the imaginations of people who've traveled long enough to exhaust their bodies. I think about how his reality intersects his myths. I don't understand, but I can accept this. I think of my father and how similar the two men are. I remember the way his feet shuffle, how he's so stubborn he won't even lift his feet. I reminisce until I fall asleep.

I know that I sleep deeply. I always sleep deeply. While I sleep, I dream myths. I dream that the woman who could be my mother takes me down the Styx. I'm not sure how I know it's the Styx. It looks like a normal river, and frankly, I'm pretty disappointed. I've always imagined it would be much darker, with souls and corpses floating around and grabbing my ankles begging for help, begging for human touch. This river isn't like that. It's a calm blue, a blue that reminds me of his eyes. The woman who could be my mother rows me to the end of the river. I wonder how a river could end, but I'm dreaming and can't articulate small details like this. A man that could be my brother approaches the canoe. I know he's supposed to represent my brother, but this man doesn't look like my brother at all. My brother is thin, practically fragile, and he's obsessively obsessed with his appearance. He runs marathons. This man has thick, oily black hair, with a large mole the size of small button under his left nostril, an exaggerated Monroe, and my brother would never look that this. My brother wouldn't step in the river like this dream-brother does. My brother wouldn't dirty his Prada shoes.

But this man that represents my brother comes closer, and he smells like shit, I mean it too, like diarrhea, and the smell is painful. He gestures an oracle, but I only want to get away from the smell so I cover my nose with my eyes. I grab the oars and paddle quickly. When I look back, he's captured the woman that could be my mother. One hand grabs her neck; the other rubs her belly. He screams, Wear good shoes tomorrow! Don't forget your strong shoes! I continue paddling and pretend to ignore him.

I paddle ferociously until I'm no longer on water. I stand in the desert, as I was standing earlier. I know it's the same place, but the plants have changed their blueprint and the land is no longer red. It is a regular desert. It looks like it could be a generic New Mexico, but it's similar enough that I'm convinced I didn't ever leave him, and then, I hear him, but he's not himself anymore. He's my father, this isn't some false representation, this is really my father, and when he moves, I hear the way my father lets his feet slide against the floor because he can't lift them any higher. I want to help him. It's a daughter's immediate reaction. I know my father isn't strong enough to hold up the burden. I know my father's been through too much, and I have to help him. I can hear him, but I can't see him. I hear him groan loudly, and I'm afraid he's fallen down.

I can't take it so I make myself wake up. I don't believe in prophetic dreams. I don't believe that dreams mean anything or that they arise from some subconscious place. I think they're just my mind having a bit of fun, replacing the familiar with the unfamiliar. I usually take pleasure in dreaming, but tonight, I'm truly tired. I decide to sleep the remainder of the night without dreams.

I wake to dense clouds, and even though I really don't believe that dreams mean anything, I sift through the two pairs of shoes I've brought and decide to wear rain boots. The roads are denser than I remember. Thick vines of lush green barricade areas that were bare sand yesterday. When the sun should be, I see a volcano emerge from a pile of pebbles. After the initial shock, the stirring mountain looks like it's been there for centuries. Little rivulets of peppery lava slither down its sides. They converge around my feet but don't touch me, almost as if the lava could be afraid to damage my plastic shoes.

On the eastern coast of Asia, "HC SVNT DRACONES" is printed in gothic lettering. There is a myth circulating that when the world was flat, many maps claimed that dragons lived near the straight edge of the earth. Of course, this isn't true.

"Here there be dragons" is only printed on one map, and it isn't even in English. It's all a myth. By the 1700s, when it was established that the earth wasn't flat, some mapmakers tried to imitate the past by creating maps claiming the existence of dragons. It was a fad. This is where "Here there be dragons" really comes from.

The dragons were supposed to protect men from wandering off the edge of the earth. If they weren't afraid of failing into the dark matter surrounding our world, maybe they would be scared of dragons.

The lava around my shoes parts as I step forward. It makes a path for me to follow. I'm unsure whether I created this road or if it's showing me which way to walk.

I follow this strange conduit, watching the landscape evolve into something entirely changed. Red rocks fold into forests. The trees puncture the sky, then dive back into the ground to emerge as rolling prairies that erupt into mountains. All of this occurs in complete silence. This natural nature lacks sound. When the lava stops moving, I hear a loud echo. He is laughing.

Strangely, his skin doesn't look as ruddy as before. I wonder if he really is a chameleon.

He is jolly. He says, I was worried that you were jesting, that you wouldn't return, but then I heard the volcano, and I knew that you'd returned.

I look at him suspiciously. I know he's lying about something.

He says, It's been a long time since I've seen another person. You know, I say that I want solitude, but I've missed the company of others. It's difficult to remain so alone for so long. Still, don't misunderstand. I don't trust you. People only come to steal things from me. The last time someone sought my company, he wanted me to steal some golden apples for him, but we all know how that story goes. He completes his seven tasks and is forever glorified, and well, here I am. So tell me stranger, what do you want from me?

I can't concentrate on what he's saying. I can only hear his feet shuffling.

I catch myself faltering and say, I dreamed of you. There's nothing else to it. I spent years training my body to hold great weights. I may look small, but my shoulders are strong. No one can hold expectation like I can.

I almost call him father.

I'm so tired of pity, he says. He says, Please go.

I try to tell him that I don't mean him any harm, that I only want to help, that I can already feel the pressure of his weight on my body, that I am used to expectations that can crush bone, but his disappointment deafens my words. Silently, with pride tucked behind my grinding teeth, I leave. I hear disparate sounds that resemble cries, but incomplete words mean nothing to me.

I go back to my hotel room. I have nowhere else to go and because I have nothing else to do while I'm there, I reexamine the photographs of the Lenox globe. The Latin lettering that once stood below the eastern coast of Asia is gone. I can see a slight indentation where the words were, like they'd been haphazardly erased. The map now looks like any other map. There is nothing special about it. I'm afraid that without the magic of dragons, I'll never be able to find him again.

Suddenly, I'm afraid that he doesn't really exist, that this entire trip has been part of an epic dream. Luckily, I don't invest in dreams.

After lunch, I decide that I have to return to him, to prove that he's real, to assuage myself. It isn't difficult for me to find him this time. Volcanoes sprout from the earth to lead my way, and as soon as my shadow touches them, they crumble under their own weight making small plateaus that continually flatten until the landscape behind me is a desert without contour.

I am close to him, I know that, but there is no laughter. There is only silence. When I actually see him, I see only a man, a plain and simple looking man, hunched over, arms up-stretched supporting a large iridescent blue stone. His skin is a clean tan, and his eyes match the rock he's holding. He isn't the man I've met before. This is an entirely changed person. For a moment, I think I've come to the wrong man. This isn't the man I was destined to help.

He says, I'm not so impressive now, am I?

He looks up at me. When he moves, he doesn't crackle. When his lips form words, they don't bound or echo. He sounds meek and quiet. He sounds submissive.

I laugh because I'm embarrassed to shake my head. I laugh because I don't want to respond, but I know that it's necessary. I say, No, no you don't look very impressive at all. In fact, you look completely foolish, and I feel kind of foolish standing her beside you. I laugh because I haven't said any of this. I laugh because I'm still shaking my head.

He inhales my movement, and I think he understands. He says, The sky, the world, all the burdens you've read about in all the stories, they're here, in this rock, smaller and less impressive than a boulder. I don't think boulder is a fair word. This is what I've been, this is what I've always been.

I say, No. I saw you before. This isn't you. I know what I saw. This isn't you. Atlas, this isn't you.

He is patient. I am confused. He is kind in his deliberation.

Listen, he says. What you saw before was what you wanted to see. You read the myths, and when you saw me, you made me. I promise you, this is it. This way. As I am now. As I will always be.

I say, I don't understand.

I can't explain it to you, he says. I can only say that you said that the dragons led you here, and you know that dragons aren't real, and you know that since that first time, you haven't seen a single dragon, and you know that you'll never see another dragon again.

He's right. I laugh because he's right, and I'm foolish. It'd never occurred to me before. I only had time to absorb all the other changes. I look at his eyes. They're the same shade as the foam that builds over salt-water waves. This must be the color of his tears.

I say, You aren't at all what I saw before, but I still see all the beauty in you.

He says, You don't think I'm a fraud?

I say, I think you're glorious.

His face winces. It distorts awkwardly. For a moment, I'm sure he's having an epileptic seizure. After a few minutes, he beams a soft smile from his blubbery pink lips. I can tell this is a new facial posture him, but it seems natural.

When he smiles, I try to hide my shock. The weight he supports shrinks again. It is the size of a medium sized rock, something large enough for one person to sit on. He doesn't even need to hold it on his shoulders. Instead, he rolls in down his arms, and by the time it reaches his hands, his burden is a small blue pebble. He divides it with his fingers, as if rock could be dough, and gives me half.

Before I can thank him, his burden multiplies exponentially. He's at ease with this and quickly shifts it back onto his shoulders. Again, he smiles, but this time, it's unnatural, a crooked chisel mark. His eyes are charcoal.

Will I ever see you again?

I don't have a response for him. He keeps on asking, wanting an answer, and every word makes the mass on his shoulders expand and elongate. The rock changes into bricks and it builds itself higher. I laugh. I don't know why, but I laugh hard.

I say, Thank you, Atlas. I say, I think I have to go now. I say, Thank you.

He mouths, Good-bye. It barely comes out.

I turn to hold his body in mine, to loop my arms through his, to alleviate his suffering, but I don't. Instead, I turn and walk away. I whisper, Bye. I tightly grab the bead of lapis lazuli he's given me.

I turn around after a few steps, but already, he's disappeared. Where he was standing, I see brick multiply and layer itself higher and higher towards the heavens, brick piling on top of more brick until it stretches miles into the sky. Where he was standing, there is a city.

o is nothing. It is not a mother, a father, or a

child. It is as empty as its center.

chapter

x:

(a quadratic story)

EQUALS: I am not the first person to say this. This is nothing new. I mean, think about it this way, right? There's a man and a woman. A man has certain anatomy, and a woman has certain anatomy, and I mean, even a blind man or an imbecile could tell you that they're not the same, and I mean, really, if two things aren't the same, how can they be equal? Ok, so I'm not quite making my point yet, right? Imagine at the very beginning, if you believe in the Bible, that is. So God created Man, and Man is Adam, and Adam was lonely so God created Eve, and He called her woman. He didn't call her Man, which means that Man and Woman aren't the same thing, and even the Bible sure as shit didn't see man and woman as equals so my question is: Why do all these people keep pushing for something that by its very definition is impossible to attain? I mean, the equality they want isn't real. It's not. As long as there is any difference at all, there's not even a chance of equality. Think about it like an equation, right? I mean, let's just take the quadratic. X equals negative B plus or minus the square root of B squared minus 4AC divided by 2A. It looks like the two sides are different, but I tell you what, if X equals 11, then the equation will equal 11. That's equality. That's equal. This man/woman shit, that's not equal. That's trying to make 10 equal 11, and I mean, it doesn't take a blind man or an imbecile to tell you how that's just wrong.

And the Father says, We need a doctor in the family, and it's your obligation to be that doctor. And the Mother says, I just want you to have enough money to support us when you get older. And the Father says, We want you to be happy, but you need to be successful. Doctors are successful. And the Mother says, Your father and I are getting older. We can't work like we used to. And the Father says, I'm not as strong as I was. I wish you lived here and could take care of me. And the Mother says, Your brother and sister don't even care for us. You're the only one we have left. And the Father says, I've invested my whole life for you. And the Mother says, Can't you come home? I worry about you. And the Father says, I miss you. And the Mother says, We don't have enough money for me to retire, but please don't send us anything. I don't want you to worry. And the Father says, Maybe one day you'll make enough to support us. And the Mother says, Maybe we can come live with you. And the Father says, I'm sick. And it is a surprising that the Daughter is continuously sad and negative about her achievements. And the Mother says, Please don't be depressed. I wouldn't want you to be depressed. I just want to love you, my baby.

Bob, being broke, but barely bad-tempered, brought brie. Brian, being bawdy, brought beachwear. Brianna brought bulletin boards. Billy, being bedridden by beestings, begged Bridget & Bridget brought Billy's baby blues.

Back behind Babylon, bachelors bask beautiful. Bachelorettes bare busting bosoms, begetting bacchanalia. Both bite, branding bodies.

Minus or Plus?

An argument

The problem is not in the graph or the mathematics of it. The problem is fundamentally a problem of language. Any number less than zero is deemed "negative" and symbolized by the "minus" sign, thereby defining that which is "minus" is negative. Of course, although "negative" in this instance is not necessarily that which is bad, undesirable, or discouraging, if a person knows this definition as the definition of the word "negative," it is absolutely impossible to forget or simply substitute some other definition; therefore, even though ideally negative numbers are mere mirrors of positive numbers, there is attached to any number with a minus sign a negative, please do pardon the pun, connotation. With this in mind, I want to ask you: Why would anyone choose Minus over Plus?

What would you get if you buried a cube of ice & let it grow?	What would you get if you dug up an ice cube?
A rooted square!	A square root!
What would get if you buried a nerd & let it grow?	What would you get if you dug up a buried nerd?
A rooted square!	A square root!

B^{2}ob^2, b^{2}eing b^{2}roke, b^{2}ut b^{2}arely b^{2}ad-tempered, b^{2}rought b^{2}rie. B^{2}rian, b^{2}eing b^{2}awdy, b^{2}rought b^{2}eachwear. B^{2}rianna b^{2}rought b^{2}ulletin b^{2}oards. B^{2}illy, b^{2}eing b^{2}edridden b^{2}y b^{2}eestings, b^{2}egged B^{2}ridget & B^{2}ridget b^{2}rought B^{2}illy's b^{2}ab^{2}y b^{2}lues.

B^{2}ob^2, b^{2}eing b^{2}roke, b^{2}ut b^{2}arely b^{2}ad-tempered, b^{2}rought b^{2}rie. B^{2}rian, b^{2}eing b^{2}awdy, b^{2}rought b^{2}eachwear. B^{2}rianna b^{2}rought b^{2}ulletin b^{2}oards. B^{2}illy, b^{2}eing b^{2}edridden b^{2}y b^{2}eestings, b^{2}egged B^{2}ridget & B^{2}ridget b^{2}rought B^{2}illy's b^{2}ab^{2}y b^{2}lues.

B^{2}ack b^{2}ehind B^{2}ab^{2}ylon, b^{2}achelors b^{2}ask b^{2}eautiful. B^{2}achelorettes b^{2}are b^{2}usting b^{2}osoms, b^{2}egetting b^{2}acchanalia. B^{2}oth b^{2}ite, b^{2}randing b^{2}odies, b^{2}aking b^{2}ab^{2}ies.

B^{2}ack b^{2}ehind B^{2}ab^{2}ylon, b^{2}achelors b^{2}ask b^{2}eautiful. B^{2}achelorettes b^{2}are b^{2}usting b^{2}osoms, b^{2}egetting b^{2}acchanalia. B^{2}oth b^{2}ite, b^{2}randing b^{2}odies, b^{2}reeding b^{2}ab^{2}ies.

Research has shown that King Midas was endowed with the gift of gold. What research has shown this, you ask? Archeologists have recently found a castle with millions of gold artifacts. When the archeologists chipped through the ground, they found thousands of bowls buried, with lips kissing tightly, as if the bowls could be lovers. Each one of the bowls and every other artifact found in the castle, when tested in the laboratory, proved to be composed to solid gold. What is most disturbing about this discovery were the thousands of men, women, and children, whose faces where emblazoned with agony. When archeologists first discovered the castle, with its multifarious artifacts, they assumed that it belonged to some king who was twisted enough to commission sculptures of people with pained looks; however, after peeling off the various layers of gold, scientists found the internal workings of real human beings, thereby proving the existence the reality of the myth of King Midas.

The myth says that King Midas was endowed with the gift of gold, but the truth of it is that the legend of King Midas is merely a romanticized version of the real horrors of Minus the alchemist.

Minus lived in the early thirteenth century. He spent most of his days silently collecting scraps of iron and tin. (Alchemy does not call for tin, which was one obvious mistake that Minus made.) After bringing all the bits of metal to a boil in a large cauldron, he used tongs to extract a jar's worth of his concoction for further experimentation, but the tongs melted, as the metal was very hot. Not thinking, Minus reached into the cauldron with his hand (and eventually his arm) in attempt to retrieve the jar. Instead of finding the glass, he withdrew an arm glazed with iron, tin, and a hint of sparking gold, which was probably a byproduct of molten tin. Still everyone insisted that his arm, despite its permanently damaged state, was made of solid gold. The arm, however, was merely gilded and lame. Minus was never able to use that arm again.

Four	For	Fore	Faure

Faure is the name of a composer. Unfortunately, it is pronounced For-Á. The author should still be commended for trying.

According to Webster's New Collegiate Dictionary, faure is a breed shorthaired domestic cat with green eyes and a cream-colored fur. Indigenous to Thailand. Extinct for nearly 50 years due to the crossbreeding of the Siamese cat. Pronounced For.

Dear Achilles,

You were named after a hero, a great hero perhaps, and of course, I am a fool and actually treated you like you were my hero. Thinking of you, my darling Achilles, made any acrid tastes in my mouth disappear. You could make me accomplish anything. I used to dream we'd go live together in some acropolis, like the real Achilles might have done, but of course, this isn't a positive letter so why should I accommodate your feelings? Achilles, I have to be honest. Yours in the only name I know of that starts with the letters AC. This may actually ~~be why I'm writing you this letter,~~ but really, I wanted to dump an acre's worth of acid on you when I found out about your little party with the B's. I know you told me you would have a few friend accompany you to Babylon, but come on Achilles, did you have to do it with that girl that looked like an acacia tree? And that guy, Brian, he doesn't have a single accolade to his name! Achilles, this is it. I mean, I didn't want to do this over a letter, but after what you've done to me, I'm sure you don't even have an acoustic nerve in your body!

Signed,
Better & Bitter Betty

Dear Achilles,

You were named after a hero, a great hero perhaps, and of course, I am a fool and actually treat you like a hero. I just wanted to thank you for taking me to Babylon with you, I think that was definitely the acme of my existence, not to be melodramatic. I've never been acquainted with such a caring and kind man. I think I fell for you as soon as you told me you work with the ACLU and how you play the acoustic guitar. I hope my perception of you is accurate, but really, I think you're an ace. I don't want to seem pushy, but I heard that you & that bitch ~~Betty aren't together anymore,~~ and if it's possible, I sure would like to accelerate our presently non-existent relationship. Let me tell you a little more about myself: I'm an activist, an actress, an acupuncturist, and I actually have a very active vocabulary. Honestly, across the board, I'm an ace too. I'd tell you about my body, but really, I hope your memory is active enough to remember it, and I think you do. Call me, Achilles!

Love,
Bare-breasted Betty

P.S. I hope you didn't think you could really accrue a woman like this!

Julia Ann sat basking in the arid sun, the writer writes. He strikes the line. ~~Julia Ann sat basking in the arid sun.~~ The writer has been writing for the entire day and this line, which he has just crossed out, is the only line that he had felt even remotely attached to. Suddenly, the writer realizes that he has had Julia Ann placed in the wrong place. He starts over, Julia Ann sits in her apartment, apartment number 2A. She chose the apartment not because it was the most comfortable or because it had the best view, but because she was fascinated by the room number. None of the other apartments she considered had both a number and a letter in it. Only this one apartment complex, (Note to self: mention later that it's hardly a complex. It's more like a series of dilapidated houses.) had her aesthetically perfect combination of letter and number. (Note to self: mention that even though it's number 2A, there's no method to the numbering. Like her apartment is actually in the basement and it's not anywhere closely connected to 2nd or A? How to show this?) Julia Anne (What should her last name be? Something clever? Something classy like Daae?) is engaged to a man named Aaron (without a last name?) who is a nationally renowned aardvark breeder. (Does that just sound silly?) The writer, now getting carried away, continues writing the story. After he finishes writing the entire story, which will be a novella, he will read it over, and tear the entire manuscript into small pieces.

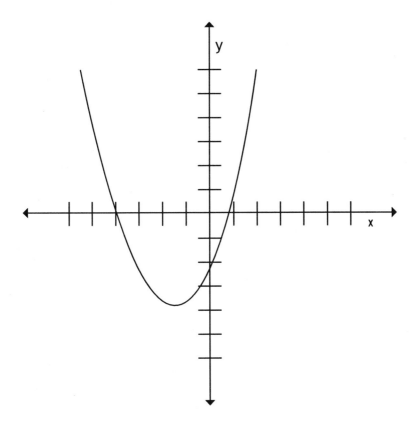

POSTSCRIPT: In order for this story to work, y must equal zero.

As the originator for all, 1 is considered both male and female. When 1 is added to male (odd), a female is produced. When 1 is added to a female (even), a male is produced. This is not a world of understanding, it is a world thriving only on addition and survival.

chapter

I

: home & place

I

HOME #5: Father lowers his head solemnly and slowly sways it from side to side. From across the kitchen table, I can only see a few freckles of black hair. The rest is white. The rest is scalp. He isn't so stern anymore. His expectations are lowered for me, and still, I disappoint him. He lifts his head momentarily, almost like he's going to speak, then it sags back down, refusing to look at me.

His feet barely lift off the floor when he walks. His calloused soles scrape against the tile, and it makes an irritating sound. He doesn't walk around the house often. Mostly, he sits in his chair, his chair from the old house, our house, smoking his pipe, using his good hand to rub feet cracked by earthquakes.

HOME #4: Father was so many things. He was an organist, a painter, a mathematician, a carpenter, a composer, but now that he is older, his titles slowly evaporate. Soon there will be no proof that he was any of these at all. As his youngest daughter, I'm forced to look away, to move away. I can't watch.

At the old Vietnamese church, a building we borrowed from the Episcopalians during their off days, Father played the organ with the choir. He rattled off the most elaborate cadences. He said, It's all tonal, my darling daughter. It isn't hard at all. He said, One day, when you're older, I'll teach you all of this. He said, This will be my gift to you. He said, This is all this poor man has to offer you.

A decade later, we acquired our own church on the south side of town. I played the violin with the church choir. Every night, Father looked over the score and composed a counter-melody. In church the next day, he'd sit back and listen closely to critique every note I played one-sixteenth out of tune. I could hear it too. I knew I would be chastised for it later. He never taught me how to compose, but I was also too busy to learn. I was too busy for him.

In my culture, parents firmly criticize their children to assure that they will do better. American children would call this kind of verbal encouragement abuse. I never questioned my parents' intentions or motives. Even today, I simply listen and obey, as any good Vietnamese daughter would do.

Our church was small, slightly larger than a shack, but every week, it was filled with a community of refugees, singing prayers to achieve the American dream. Even though I was a member of the choir, I didn't make any friends there. I was uncomfortable speaking their language, and although I was as fluent as most of the adults, I only spoke English. Between songs, I heard them say that I wasn't one of them. I heard them say that I thought I was better than them.

Every night after church, Mother would ask me if I made any new Vietnamese friends. I was too ashamed to say that they repulsed me with their thick accents and judgmental gawks. I didn't want to tell her that they didn't want me to be their friend. I never mentioned how they made a clique, and I was too American for them. So I didn't say anything. Father would tell her to hush. He would say, Our daughter is too white to make friends with her own people. Father doesn't speak often, but when he does, it stings.

HOME #2: Mother and Father return to the homeland every few years. They can only afford the plane tickets. They look to us, their children, to give them spending and giving money. It's tradition to give money, newly printed money at that, as a present when you return.

In Vietnam, American bills are worth more than their equivalent exchange. Anything American represents wealth. Cousins and distant Family walk around showing off their crisp dollar bills, smiling with their dirty, crooked teeth.

Every time, Parents ask me to return to the homeland with them. Really, I have no right to call it the homeland. I was born here. I've never been there, but I promise Mother that I'll go back sometime soon. I'm ashamed to admit that I'm afraid to go back. I'm scared that they'll laugh at me with my American accent and ask how much money I make and expect something from me. I'm not sure that this will happen, but I don't want that kind of judgment. I don't want that kind of burden.

PLACE #7: It's cold here. The walls are bare and white. It smells of sanitation.

HOME #1: Father was from the North; Mother was from the South. He spent his childhood by candlelight. He tells me the same myths.

Father says, When I was a boy, I was so poor that I couldn't afford to buy even a used book. Father says, I didn't complain like you complain though. That was my life, and you can't complain about your life. God gave you life, your mother and your father gave you life, and for that, you must always be thankful. Father says, I used to copy entire books by hand. He says, That's why my eyes are weak. Because I had to copy so many books by candlelight.

I'm not sure that I believe this story entirely, but I do know that Father used to take away my graphing calculator from me when I did my Calculus homework. He thinks that calculators are cheating devices. Father can still tell you the square root of any number less than two hundred without even a pause of hesitation.

HOME #4: Father builds for the church. Every Sunday, patrons accost us hoping to take us to lunch or dinner to thank Father for his beautiful carpentry. Mother is so proud.

HOME #1: Mother doesn't tell me about her childhood, not even myths like Father tells me. The only hint I learned about her youth came from Grandmother. Grandmother told me how they were very poor, and she sold my mother's faith to the Catholic Church. My grandmother converted two of her children for enough money to feed her entire family for weeks.

Parents don't like to tell stories of their lives before they met each other. It makes me wonder if they existed before then at all.

HOME #2: Father moved from Hanoi to Saigon, back when it was still called Saigon, to marry a thin woman with thick long hair. He forgot his dreams of being an artist to earn adequate money to make a family.

Vietnamese families live in the same house. A single residence often holds three or more generations, babies and Grandparents smiling tenderness.

It's expected that sons will bring their wives home to live with the parents, and the daughter will move in with her husband's family. Because Father's family lived in the

North, over-taken by Communism, Mother and
Father had their own home, but Mother's family
lived within a few footsteps.

He began teaching calculus at a local university. He earned a reputation
as a difficult but worthwhile professor. Unlike this country, Father was
respected and well paid as a teacher. They lived in a two-story house,
with a stucco fence and an indoor bathroom. Mother worked for the
government, taking sabbaticals to birth Sister and Brother.

PLACE #7: It isn't true. So much of this is a myth. Father wasn't really
a professor. He was a teacher. For so long, I believed he taught at the
college level, but in reality, he taught middle school students, but he
did teach them calculus.

   I think I've romanticized my father my entire life. When I look
for approval, I look to him. It isn't that I don't care for my mother. It's
that I know that she'll love me without conditions, and my father is
harder to impress. He is a one of the seven Herculean tasks.

HOME #4: The house where I grew up had three bedrooms and one
bath. It was small and brimming with memories. Father changed
everything that was square into something that was oval.

Grandmother, Aunt Five, Uncle Five, and
Cousin live one backyard away from our
backyard. Uncle Six, Aunt Six, and Cousins live
five houses to our left. Uncle Seven, Aunt Seven,
and Cousins live one block and three houses to
our left. Rightfully, Grandmother should live
with Uncle Seven, he is the youngest, but Aunt
Five insists that she live with her family.

A shed stands erected in the backyard. Our dog is buried under the
oak tree next to it. Father built the shed to store his wood working tools
and lawn mowers, but I used to play on its second tier, pretending it
was a tree house or even my own little home separate from Family.
Often I would worry about how I could survive winter without heat.
I didn't notice that every few hours, I'd still need to go inside to use
the bathroom and eat.

HOME #3: When Sister was six and Brother was five, Mother and Father fled the homeland, fled Communism and war. I've heard so many stories about the pains of travel, but I was too young to appreciate their sacrifice. I can't even remember if they traveled by plane or boat. They don't tell me those stories anymore. They think I don't care to hear.

Family landed in Pennsylvania. Grandmother, Mother, Father, Aunt Five, Uncle Five, Brother, and Sister burrowed a small hole, trying to hide from the cold. After just one month of Pennsylvania winter, Grandmother, Aunt Five, and Uncle Five migrated south to Texas permanently. They needed a warmer place, a place closer in temperature to the homeland.

Without the comfort of Family, Mother and Father spent their days cleaning laundry for people with too much money to do it themselves and evenings learning English. Father speaks four languages: Vietnamese (two dialects), Latin, French, and English, but the English he learned was a written English, a textbook English, never spoken, never heard, so even though he could conjugate any verb, he couldn't sound out a full sentence.

HOME #4: Mother used to ask me, Are a you a Vietnamese girl or an American girl? Proudly, I would answer, Con la nguoi Vietnam. She'd smile, hug me warmly, and say, Me thuong con qua. I run up to Father and yell, Con la nguoi Vietnam! Em be Bo la nguoi Vietnam!

I didn't understand why he didn't tell me he loved me like Mother did.

HOME #3: Brother and Sister went to elementary school. One day, the neighbor that was supposed to let them into the apartment wasn't home. Sometimes, when Mother tells this myth, the woman went to the hospital. Other times, she was out shopping. The hospital is much more romantic, much more reasonable, but realistically, she probably accidentally forgot about them and went shopping for new shoes. The way Mother tells the story, Sister needed to go the bathroom and didn't know what to do so she pissed herself and Brother was so cold from the snow that he huddled beside the door, hoping heat from the inside would crawl between wood and cement to give him warmth. Parents return home from work to see

Children with frosted eyelids. The way Mother tells the story, that night, that very night, they packed their few belongings and began their travels south to rejoin Mother's family in Texas. Mother says that she wanted sun and family to melt all the fear and sadness from her children's minds.

HOME #2: Father walks around with his digital camcorder that Brother bought him to document his trip to the homeland. He gets sick the first week. According to Mother, the water in Vietnam isn't safe. If I ever go back, I should never eat fruit unless I wash it myself. Also, I should eat food if I see it cooked directly in front of me. According to Mother, even in Saigon, you need to be careful what you eat. She says, Our bodies aren't like their bodies. She says, We aren't as strong anymore. I don't ask her if I was ever that strong.

On their return, Father sits me down in front of the huge flat-screen TV Brother bought him to watch football games. Scenes of a foreign land attack my senses. I can almost smell incense and tranquility when I see the Buddhist temples. I almost feel a kinship when Mother starts naming Family I will never meet. They are incredibly thin from malnourishment and still so beautiful.

PLACE #7: I've decorated. There are some paintings on the walls; pictures clutter flat spaces; books overpower shelves. Brother bought me a new comforter. At night, I wrap myself like a summer roll.

At home, Mother cooks for me. Father washes my dishes. I'm alone here. I have to provide for myself. Often, I call Mother for recipes, but my food lacks the light spices of affection. They spoil me, my family. It's hard to imagine them so far away. Once, when I was little, Mother went on a business trip to Washington DC, and she was gone for maybe a week. During that week, I pretended that she had died, and at night, I cried so hard because I couldn't remember her face, I couldn't remember what it felt like to hug her. Father thought I missed her. He completely misunderstood my tears.

I don't cry here. I think the sterility may have dried up my tear ducts.

HOME #2: In Saigon, Parents had many pets before Siblings were born. Father's always been a lover of animals; Mother is allergic to everything.

Once, Father brought home a small puppy, handsome brown spots on a white body, along with a luxurious leather couch to bribe Mother into letting him keep his new toy.

Traditional Vietnamese families are extremely patriarchal and agist. The only exception to complete male domination over the family appears when someone from an older generation also lives with the family, and regardless of gender, that person rules the house. When I ask Mother about gender roles, she tells me, Well of course the man rules the family. If you look at every Eastern culture, the women are submissive. That's how they're attractive to the men. Look at me, she says. She says, Anything I do, I have to ask your father first. That's just the way it is. It's the right way to be. I try to explain to her that what she described isn't really the way it is, not even in our family, but she doesn't understand the term passive-aggressive and she doesn't understand the *American* concept of manipulation so she just plays dumb, and because she's my elder, I say nothing else. Also, traditional Vietnamese women defer their intelligence to their male or older counterparts.

The way Father tells it, Mother has a soft spot for things that cost money. So did the puppy, and when Mother saw her furniture destroyed, she forced Father to get rid of the dog.

Giving it to the postman, Father pet his petite head. Later that week, the postman invited Father over for stew. Rage punched the man, not Father.

HOME #5: When I was twenty, the loneliest disease fortified Mother's colon. Being so alone, it multiplied a colony to torture her. With friends, it flourished, and no amount of chemotherapy or radiation could chase it away.

Tired and sore, Mother asked Father for a new home. Father can't say no to her. It's not within his abilities to deny her anything she wants.

They didn't ask my opinion, but they knew that I didn't agree with the move. Parents don't have enough money to purchase a new home. With Mother sick and Father retired, I didn't know how to tell them they couldn't afford it. I didn't want to remind them how they're retirement age. Like a good Vietnamese daughter, I kept quiet and submitted to my parents' wants.

So again, Parents packs their rucksacks, larger now than before, and migrated twenty miles north. Mother received another two-story house from Father.

HOME #3: Brother and Sister were embarrassed. Unable to articulate needs and wants, they tacitly sat in seats too large and looked at the woman in the front of the classroom with awkward shaped eyes. At lunch, they didn't eat sandwiches and applesauce like the other kids. Caste to the far corner of the cafeteria, they unpacked rice and beef stew, cold from hours of sitting in crammed backpacks.

Now that they have decades dividing them from these memories, they deny their culture. They deny their entire past. They've forgotten the language they grew up speaking and only eat Vietnamese food out of novelty. Mother and Father often tell me how they dreamed their life here would be. Mother and Father often tell me that all those dreams are now transferred onto me because Brother and Sister have disappointed them, have failed them. Impossible as they are, I know I must meet their expectations.

PLACE #7: Mother calls me daily, asking me if I've made any Vietnamese friends. I try to explain that there isn't a booming Vietnamese population in the Midwest and how I'm so busy with school that I don't have time to find them, but those are all lies. I haven't tried. I speak with Father once a week. Our conversations don't stray far from comfortable subjects like football or school. If he asked me about the future, he knows he'd be disappointed, and he'd rather not know than have me, his youngest, be the cause of his sadness.

Parents don't understand what I study. To them, there are only three branches in the academy: medicine, law, and engineering.

Liberal arts aren't mentioned because they can't offer success by their definition, and their definition is rooted in the American dream. Their definition is an expensive German car, two-story house kept safe by a white picket fence, and of course, little blonde children. Parents have two sets of dreams, and they contradict each other.

I spend hours remembering the homes of my past. I spend even more time dreaming of all the homes my parents and siblings have seen, lived in, called their own. I'm worried that now that I'm so far from Parents, I may not ever call this place home.

HOME #4: Father enrolled me in language class when I was nine. Although I had a more complex vocabulary than all the other kids, I could barely even read menu items. I didn't make friends with my classmates. Back then, I was too young to be embarrassed by my culture. I was simly too awkward to make friends of any nationality.

HOME #5: Father's heart stopped pumping. Mother frantically called all Family. I was nowhere near home, and by the time I was reached, Father was connected to machines from every artery and vein. Brother nodded at me, explaining everything in too medical terms. Mother's eyes wouldn't dry.

Father forgot how to walk. He couldn't use his right hand, the hand he used to paint and write when he was angry, and his left hand, the hand he used to write when he was happy and the hand that holds his chopsticks, was numb and weak, but still functional. Mother spent months crawling in my twin sized bed while Father relearned childhood skills. I'm embarrassed to admit that her presence annoyed me. I wanted her to be strong. I wanted her to be independent. I didn't want her to depend on me.

When Father came home, he slept downstairs. He couldn't walk up stairs so high. Unable to work outside in his garden or occupy himself with woodworking, Father declined into melancholy. Mother's medication made her dolor. Worried about Father and her own cancer, she stopped taking care of herself. She couldn't eat. She lost all her body fat except in her belly, which protruded grandly. Her doctors prescribed her anti-depressants. She even know what she was taking. Her doctors prescribed her medicinal marijuana. She didn't know what that was either. When I told her, she refused to touch it. Father took sleeping pills to make it through the night, but artificial sleep didn't wake his body when he needed to urinate. Every morning, Mother would scrub the futon downstairs and do a load of laundry. Father was embarrassed. We never spoke about it.

I spent my time avoiding home. I'd go anywhere to not be there. I couldn't watch my parents in their sadness and decay. Parents couldn't understand. Perhaps they never will.

PLACES #1-6: Sister moved away when I was still in elementary school. She moved from man to man, each one disgracing her further through Parents' eyes. Brother lived at home until recently. He's twelve years older than me. He didn't move out until he was well into his thirties. He was supposed to be their pride, the male, the descendant. He went through decades of schooling, then he quit. He was so close to being called doctor. Parents haven't forgiven him for this. He moved out to hide from their judgments about his education, his life, his homosexuality.

I am the main link between Parents and Siblings. I am the peacekeeper. Every time I talk to Siblings, I want to tell them to appreciate Parents. Every time I talk to parents, I am frustrated. As the youngest, I can't say anything to anyone.

In Vietnamese culture, one can't argue to those older than her. It's considered disrespectful. Like other Asian cultures, we believe wisdom comes with years. A younger person must always heed the advice of her elders. I've met few Americans who can sympathize.

Sister has moved across the country to follow her military man. With two children and two dogs, they pretend to be happy, unquestioning, content. Brother remains in the same city as Parents, but he's more distant than the miles of Sister and me added together. He lives only fifteen minutes south with Partner. They pretend to be happy, unquestioning, content. They are all-American. They've achieved Parents' American Dream.

HOME #2: Mother and Father leave for the homeland this January. Mother wants me to go this time. She's afraid it'll be their last vacation.

I'm skeptical and worried. They're weak. Father can walk but he sways from side to side, trying to find equilibrium. Father can't tell when he needs to go the bathroom. Mother constantly asks him if he needs to urinate. He always says no, and suddenly, he needs to go and can't wait and there's a stain on his pants. Mother runs to the bathroom after every meal. Often, she shits in her panties. She can't imprison disease in her fading body.

I've promised them that when I'm done with school, I'll journey with them, as a family. I've promised this for nearly ten years, but this time, I mean it. I know they're fading, and I have to go with them, for them.

HOME #5: Mother rubs Father's feet every night after he washes the dishes. Her medication causes coldness to burn her skin. She can't open the refrigerator, let ice cubes chill her water, walk outside in the winter.

Now that I'm gone from the house, Parents spend most of their evenings with Uncle Six, Aunt Six, and their family. They have five slit-eyed grandbabies sliding over tiled floors. Mother is getting ready to retire, allowing governmental compensation for her illness to give her the luxury of life without eleven hours of work per day. She's been talking about retiring for years. Father spends his days outside building different structures for the new church. He's better, but it still takes him months to complete projects that once took him weeks to finish.

Parents are more than content. They are loving and happy.

PLACE #7: People who don't share my past, my culture, my beliefs surround me. Often, I want nothing more than a friend who looks like me to tell that she understands, but as lonely as I am here, I would rather hide from the truth of how sick my parents are than confront reality. Parents would rather boast about the name of my school rather than tell people what I study. I'm alone, and I remain a failure to Parents.

HOME #6: Father laughs heartily, gently patting my back. His hair has no black left in it. Mother places a wrinkled hand against her blackened face, another side-affect of the chemo. Brother, increasingly thin, sits across from me, next to Sister. Her hair is dyed golden brown and it's been curled at the edges. Brother is a doctor. I am a doctor. Sister is a housewife and proud mother. Mother and Father are healthy again. We join together as Family in our home.

Parents pray for this daily.

In religious traditions, 2 is the disunion, the falling apart of absolute unity, but it is also the world of creation, as every creature is twofold in itself.

Some religious mathematicians once believed that 2, like 1, was also not a real number. They reasoned that 1 + 1 = 2; however, the primordial One cannot be repeated or cloned. To them, 2 was sacrilegious.

chapter 2: the unknown

Let me tell you a story, she says.

I'm really nervous, I say. I tell her, This is my first time, and I don't really know what I'm doing.

She's kind. Her skin is dark and wrinkled, and I'm strangely comfortable with her because of this. I want to trust her. I want her to give me answers.

She says, I am an old woman, dear girl, and I've been doing this a very long time. Each wrinkle on my face is a fortune I've told, and I'm always correct. I tell you, I am one of the last great fortunetellers. I am part of a dying breed, like barren chicken, but this is not a story about me, my child. I want you to relax. You are full of anxiousness. Breathe. Calm yourself. Listen to my voice, and trust. Always trust.

I want to believe her, but I'm skeptical. I say, What makes you one of the last great fortunetellers?

She says, I am great because I am seasoned in every method of telling. I draw on every tradition to tell your fate, but surely, my child, all of this you will soon see. Now my child, come and relax. Take my hand and remember to breathe.

I say, I trust you.

She says, No, you don't. But you will.

I say, How do you know?

Your eyes, she says. Your eyes are the color of the shadows of cacti without flowers.

I think that's beautiful and smile shyly. She says, Now, you begin to trust me, and child, it is time to begin. Give me your right hand. Close your eyes.

She says, In your hand, I am placing a deck of cards. Without opening your eyes, divide this deck of cards in half and then in half again. When you are done, put the pieces back together. Good. Now, cover the entire deck with your left hand. Good. Good.

The cards are old and worn. Threads of paper are soft against my fingers. I want to pull them apart and forget all of this, but then I think of my Herr Doktor and I can't. I think of the way he awkwardly shuffles the paper in the morning, stopping periodically to inspect a photograph. I want the courage to talk to him. I want so much.

You can open your eyes, she interrupts. She says, Please, my child, turn over the first card and place it on the table. Oh my! Yes, well, it's all right, my dear girl. It isn't nearly as bad as it seems.

I'm confused. I don't know why this card is so terrible, and I want to beg her to explain. I want her to be kind.

She says, Let me tell you a story that I think may clarify things for you. Perhaps in all this murkiness, together, we can find our way through the fog.

There is a man, she says. He is a young man, but his teeth retain the shadows of dark coffee. His smile is gentle, and you find joy in it. There is something very caring about him, and you look for him every day. I'm unsure how you see him daily, but you both manage to find time for each other. Of course, you should know that you are his day, but yes, this is very strange. You don't know him, do you, my child? Yes, you two don't know each other, but you both dream. In your dream, he takes your hand, and you notice how soft his hands are. Beneath his fingernails are remnants of blue and orange paint. You remember this because these are lovely colors to you, and from that day forward, you wear nothing but those two colors. In your dream, from that day on, you don't have another day without him. I tell you, my child, his dreams are not so different. In his dream, you wear a black dress. Your hair floats as you sashay into a room filled with lights and cameras. As your picture is taken, he yawns, fearful that some other man will steal you from him. In his dream, he cherishes you, but he is perpetually concerned that you will somehow be too good for him. Even while dreaming, he is insecure.

Of course, my child, she says, there is so much danger in living in dreams. This young man, he has invested too much of his time in this dream, and when he is awake, he can no longer recognize you from your dream self. He sits and watches you, hoping that you will suddenly become the woman he sleeps with every night after he has fallen asleep. This is his pleasure, not yours.

In the daylight, you are left with only pain, but do not fear, my child, the six of cups is a strange and powerful card. You see, when one cup exceeds its limits, it overflows into the next cup and so on and so forth until all the cups are so full of pleasure and satisfactions that the entire world will become saturated with physical joy. Now, that doesn't seem so terrible, does it?

I say, No, but tell me. Does he love me or does he not? What will happen?

Her smile is patient, understanding. She says, You are rushing. Imagine each card is a metronome, and you must keep in time. You are a musician, no? You understand my meaning.

I say, How did you know?

She doesn't answer. It's unnecessary. I want to ask her how she knew about him. I'm sure she has a way. I know that this is some kind of clever scheme. She isn't really a fortuneteller. She just tells stories well. She can read me somehow.

She says, Child, stay with me. She says, You're wandering. I understand. It is time to have faith. Please, turn the next card.

I hadn't noticed before, but this room isn't at all what I expected a fortuneteller's room to look like. She's surprisingly urban. Everything in this room is new and framed. Every object has a purpose. There aren't any knickknacks. I'm sure it isn't a requirement, but I always assumed that a fortuneteller would have spare knickknacks just sitting around. I imagined the room would be cluttered and messy, maybe even dark, a little musty perhaps. There's no dust in this room. There's nothing unclean in this entire room. I flip over the next card.

She says, I'm glad you've returned. You're just in time for another story. It's a tale about a young woman. Once, there was a kind and beautiful woman, with curves that find their way into men's dreams. She possesses a magical power in her dark eyes. Always, her eyes look shadowed, although she would never use color or powder to taint her face. Despite her beauty, or perhaps because of it, this young woman lacked confidence in all aspects of her life. She hardly retained enough surety to decide what clothing to wear in the morning. She never completed school because she was always taught to value only beauty. People constantly told her she was stupid, but at least she had a nice face, and beauty makes up for everything else. This young woman didn't want to believe that her fate was that of a trophy wife, but so many people had told her that she believed it. She was convinced that she had no other qualities, and as such, she could hardly pick out clothes in the morning.

But then, something amazing happened. One day, as she was desperately trying to choose between a paisley and a plaid skirt, she noticed something odd on her palm. She'd never noticed it before, but there were small lines on her hand. That day, she didn't leave her closet. She spent the entire day tracing the indentations on her palm. That day, she fell in love with herself. From that day on, she dedicated herself to the study of palmistry. Of course, she slowly moved beyond just that, but it all started with a frightening decision between plaid and paisley.

She laughs. She says, You think I'm telling my story.

I say, Yes. I think you just told me your life story, how you got to this point.

You are confused, my child, she says. She says, I've already told you. This story is not about me. This is all about you. It is undeniable that because I am telling your story, it is possible that my own past and future could become entangled in yours, but I am certain that there exists wisdom in my words. Let me see your right hand. It was with the hand, after all, that I began my life. Perhaps I can help you begin your life here as well.

To be polite, I extend my hand. Her skin is cold and leathery. I want to jolt my hand free.

She begins, Once, there was a young man, and he was quite handsome.

I retreat my hand. I ask, Are all of the people in your stories attractive? What happens if there's an ugly person?

She is calm. She says, My child, you are beautiful. Everything you touch receives some of that beauty. Now, give me your hand again.

She says, His eyes are the color of sorrow, and he's trained as a surgeon, although his hands have rarely touched flesh. I don't know how this can be, but I'm quite sure of it. I know this sounds quite odd, but I assure you, he is exactly as I've described.

Yes, she says, as a young man, he was very lonesome. Although the world greeted him with success, he remained alone and sad. Then one day, oh, oh, it's terrible. There is a shortness here. No, his parents were killed in a most unfortunate accident. It was a car accident, involving many parties, but they were the only ones truly harmed. I can't tell how many there were. The lines are too blurry for me to read, but I am sure that this young man grew into an adult with a great sum of money.

I say, I don't understand what this story has to do with me. I say, Is this his story? My Herr Doktor?

She says, I cannot say for certain. I only know that this is the story written on your hand. It is etched in your skin, part of your fabric, it is the story of your life. My child, there is no need for you to look at me with such suspicion. Of course, I don't mean that it's literally your life story. I only want to help tell you the unknown that you search for. I've told you what your palm wanted you to know.

Using her middle finger, she traces a line on my hand. Her fingertip is warm.

She says, You see this line here? This is the line where it all started. This is the first pulse, the first glance, the first hint of knowledge. In this line, I see a sadness my words can't capture. It tells a tale of loneliness that most can never know. There is a man who has traveled the earth. He is a nomad, gathering the memories of people who have cried for most of their lives. He takes their stories in his hands, and using his pointer finger and his thumb, he rolls them into smooth cylinders. Then he coils them tights, like a cinnamon roll without sugar. Clamping his eyes, he opens his lips to the memories and swallows loudly. In his belly, thousands of tears are trapped, and the people he has seen are stripped of their rightful sorrow. He is a thief, and I don't want you to misunderstand my words. He does not remove sorrow out of altruism. Rather, he wants to harness pain in his body so he can be in a state of constant desolation.

You wonder why this appears in your palm, she says. My child, your eyebrows are shifting in a most uncomfortable manner. You are worried that this is your fate. I must tell you the truth, my dear, I don't know if this is your future. I can only read what has been engraved in your skin, a ritual of unmasking the unknown, making the commonplace the extraordinary.

She's misunderstood my concern. I'm frustrated. She's supposed to offer answers, and she can't even tell that I'm not concerned for myself. She is a fraud.

I say, You've misunderstood.

No, my child, she says, you've misunderstood. I wish you would stop assuming that I am a fraud.

How did you know? I ask.

I am not stupid, dear girl. I can watch your face and understand many things. For instance, even while I was speaking, you were overly concerned that every word I spoke was a condemnation against the man you love. You were worried that I was telling his fate. You see, my dear, I think you have entirely misunderstood what I do. I cannot tell someone's fate. I am a storyteller. I take what is offered to me, whether it is a card or your skin, and I translate it into your life. So my child, if this is his fate, I did not tell it. If this is his past, it has somehow been written onto your body. It is as though you have eaten some of his sorrow and his tears have carved channels through your flesh. Do you see this line here? There are thousands of small gashes, each representing an irreconcilable pain.

But enough of sadness, she says. She says, I am sure that I am not necessary to tell you how you already feel, but of course, if you could truly feel all of this, you would not have come here to me today, would you?

I shake my head. I trust her. I fear her.

You lack the ability to wade through your own emotions. Your body, she says, has become a rainforest, and your eyes have become swollen from the swarming bugs. Leeches have attached themselves to your throat, and you cannot speak. I know you are afraid, and I am here. I am here to painlessly remove the gauzy drapes that veil your vision. I am here to help. Let me offer you a cup of tea.

As soon as she leaves, I'm tempted to rummage through her belongings. I want to find her secrets, but more than that, I want to believe her. I want her to tell me what my future will be with my sweet Herr Doktor. I'm ashamed that I don't know his name. I've watched him, poured his coffee for him, dreamt about him, but I know so little about him. In truth, I hate him. He should have had the courage by now to approach me. In truth, by now, I should've had the courage. I want her to give me that. I need her to tell me this is right.

My child, she interrupts, you are in thought. I'm setting your tea here, and in your left hand, I'm setting a cylinder. Close you eyes again for me. I want you to shake it slowly. You'll here it rattle. That's natural. Don't be afraid. Stop being so tentative. Live, my girl!

The cylinder is rough. Its texture is interesting. I want to rub it rather than shake it.

That's it, she says. This is all I needed. You can stop shaking.

I hold on to the canister. I don't want her to take it away. I'm surprised that she doesn't even try to. There's something magical about this can.

She says, Look at me. Look deeply, she says. In me, there is reflection of you. I am part of you. When you released this hexagram, a fraction of me fell from the can as well. You look at me as though you can't understand what I am saying. Let me explain. She says, I can feel your 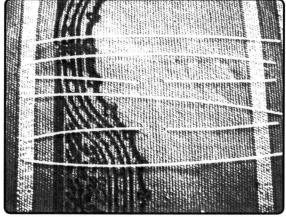 sadness, and although I can't tell what causes this great sorrow, I move closer to this and to you.

I say, I'm sorry.

You don't need to be sorry, my child. I just need for you to be more confident. Let me tell you a story. Would you like it to be a story of the man or the woman? No. No. Don't answer. The hexagram has already spoken for you, and it dictates that this should be the tale of a woman, constantly struggling with a smile.

Once there was a woman. This woman could be you. She could even be me. You must understand that even in stories there is flexibility in character. It matters not who she is because she is not really any woman. She has sapphire eyes that flood her face. She has had a difficult life. Most days, she eats little but speaks to excess. She spends her entire day speaking to herself. There is no one else for her to converse with.

When she was a child, she had no friends. Her parents often took her to therapists because she refused to speak in school, but the moment she arrived in the safety of her bedroom, she would maintain self-dialogues for hours, never stopping for food or drink. She seldom stopped until the sun rose and the school bus arrived. Her parents had no experience on how to handle a situation such as this. Her therapists spoke with her and diagnosed her with strange Latin words that filled a page from side to side. They stuck electricity into her frail body, and still, she wouldn't speak. After a decade of this sort of medication, she walked into a café and asked for a job. Those were the first words she'd spoken in public for over twenty years.

The hexagram you have released tells the story of time through patience. Although I've already told you the story, let me speak just a little longer, my child. You are a silent type. I can tell. The man you love also hides his words. You see him every day, but you lack the ability to vocalize your feelings. I assure you that he also cannot speak what he feels. This is a story about patience and time. Let water weave its way into your heaven. Time and evolution cannot be rushed, but this is only part of what you need to know.

She takes my teacup. Her movement is rushed. I feel her excitement.

You've waited long, my child. You have waited and waited, and you can't wait for me to finish so that you can know, but things are not always so simple.

She picks up my teacup again. She says, It's amazing what a little bit of tea can reveal. This is nothing so visceral as your palm or a card, but in many ways, this is far more potent. When remains in this cup are the substances that your body has caste aside, bits of tea deemed unworthy by harsh lips. This is what has been rejected.

Have you become bored by my stories? She asks, Do they lack the entertainment value of a movie? I will try to make this one more exciting. Of course, I can only tell what the leaves whisper in shapes foreign to your eyes.

I feign laughter.

I am told that in the mountains of Mongolia, she says, there are animals that cannot stop weeping. They are infected with something that they cannot see or feel. It is a silent and invisible murderer. You see, because these animals can't stop crying, slowly, their bodies lose water that cannot be rejuvenated because they can't stop crying for long enough to replenish their bodies. They cry until they die of dehydration. It's a long process and extremely painful. Often, yaks and goats are heard bellowing songs of torture. The villagers can do nothing to assuage them. There is no cure. It is unknown how this fatal illness spread, but it manages to extinguish entire species from the mountain's landscape. Eventually, the animals that do escape the sickness are left mourning. In the mountains of Mongolia, tears are always accompanied by the fear that ducts will forever swell with saltine sadness.

You wonder why the leaves have told me this story? You fear that this is your fate, but by now, I'm sure you know that I can't tell you your fate. I can do nothing so fantastic. I can, however, help you unravel this cloudy story, if you will allow me.

She says, Because you drank from this cup and these leaves have touched your mouth, they stand at the bottom of the cup as a reminder of your past. You are a villager eavesdropping on the wailing yaks, and you feel helpless. Perhaps this man that you love is that yak. Perhaps he is a goat. Either way, you must act. Whether he is goat or yak, if you truly love him, you must stop his pain. There is no cure for this disease. You must find it.

The leaves I read are those that were rejected. Your body finds their texture unsuitable. Let me state it more simply: This is not your fate. This is the opposite of your fate. You are not destined to be the villager and your love will not die of sadness and tears, but you must act swiftly. He is already speaking of Mongolia.

Of course, I have only told you what to do, she says. I have not answered your question, the question you came here to answer. The unknown has not been revealed, but you have not told me your question, yet I can try to find a response.

She hands me a plastic sphere. It's cold and unused.

She says, I want you to look into this ball. It's nothing fancy, but it can do many things that I am incapable of offering you. Think your question and you will have all your answers. Hold it tightly in your right hand. Turn it a full rotation and look deeply into it. It holds everything unknown.

Perhaps because 2 was not real or perhaps because Eve made 2 innately evil, 3 came to save the day. 3, also known as the Triad, leads to a new integration, one that does not negate duality but boldly overcomes it.

Lao-Tzu said that the Tao produces unity, unity produces duality, duality produces trinity, and the triad produces all things else.

Aristotle believed that 3 was the first number to which the term "all" could be rightfully applied.

Plato wanted to build a world out of triangles.

chapter

3

Δ:
(a story in verse)

3

Delta: n. [1. lit., < Gr. Delta, of Sem. orig. as in Heb. Daleth. 4th letter of the alphabet, lit. door] 1. the fourth letter of the Greek alphabet (Δ, ∂) 2. something in the shape of a delta (Δ); specif., a deposit of sand and soil, usually triangular, formed at the some of some rivers

The symbol Δ is used in mathematics to symbolize change in a variable (x, y, z).

One should not fail to notice that the letter delta forms an isosceles triangle, with two sides of equal length and two angles of equal degrees. One side (and its corresponding angle) is noticeably different, left out, uninvited.

I'm unworthy of your love
God Eve! How many times do have to go through this?
                              I mean, come on
        No, you come on! Every time we fight, you remind
                                that I was made from you
You're unbelievable
        You're unbelievable. You're a total hypocrite
You're unreasonable
        I'm unreasonable? You believe in God
Not this again
        Oh look at me! I'm Adam and I'm upset! I huff and
                        puff because I'm oh so mad
You're so fucking annoying
        And you just said I was your equal

BARTERED WORDS IN THE MIDDLE OF MIDNIGHT,
CONVERSATION #48

Isn't that what you wanted to hear
        You're such a liar
Face it, Eve, love is a lie
        No, love's an emotion
Emotions lie to be understood
        You lie to be loved
You don't get it, do you
        Yeah, I do. When you named me woman, you
                        wanted me to be below you
And I was right, you are
        And you, Adam, you're only human

It wasn't always this way. The disputes of love and equality weren't always this aged. It's her fault. Before she was made, there was another. She was the origin of love. I told her she was my equal, but she didn't accept this, and not the way Eve doesn't accept things. Lilith was logical. She made sense. If I ever said the word equal, she'd say, My darling, Adam, you're such a fool. Equality doesn't exist. There is always a less and a more. Two objects, seemingly similar in size and stature, will prove to be either superior or inferior. The moment on shows any sign of defect, the mirage of equality will evaporate like a drop of dew, struggling to drip from a wilting leaf. Choose your role carefully. Would you prefer to be the water, soon to be transformed and forever forgotten, or the leaf, looking at its own mortality

in the mirror of the earth? My darling, that's what equality is. Why should we even pretend our love is equal?

I couldn't argue with her. She was right. We weren't equal. I was hers, and she was free.

One day, a breeze violently flew her away. God gave her Free Will, and she took it.

Lilith wasn't even mortal. Even her beauty was complex. She was a mythical creature. I cradled and nurtured her. I tried to capture her, to keep her in my garden, but I am not as strong as she is. I used to believe we were all the same—me, her, Him, His countless minion—each possessing characteristics that the others desired, but life is not so simple now. He gave her the chance and replaced absolute perfection with modified perfection.

Her skin a blanket
Hiding (im)perfections

I can taste the salt of her myth

Her fingers fondle the petals of a lily
Its skin not as soft as hers

I envy that flower
      Touching her
Being Touched by her

She gave it all her love
And left me
With that blooming bud never browning
To despise
Instead of a kiss

— CLASSIFICATIONS —

GENUS & SPECIES:	Lilium lancifolium (more commonly known as Tiger Lily)
FAMILY:	Liliaceae
SOME COMMON TRAITS:	Stem over 1 m tall, scabrous, purplish
	Several flowers, nodding, the pedicels pubescent, 6-12 cm long, bracteate
	Perianth parts orange or orange-red, spotted with dark purple
	Some hybrid species known to cause hallucinations if ingested

I offered him   my body   that was   not enough
                my mind   not enough
                my God   not enough
He didn't want to own me   not enough
He wanted to be me **SACRIFICE**   enough

But that
I could not offer him

Adam, I said, I have given you everything. I'm finished giving. I'm ready to receive.

THE ULTIMATUM UNANSWERED

He was silent. A tear dwindled near the crevice of his eyes but dared not roll down onto the earth. Gravity lost its strength. He would not bow to me.

Rough patch of
Coarse hair
DELTA
Warmth
Sated
Me

Come on, Adam. Be honest. Tell me you still love
her
Who
You know who
Right
Well do you? Go ahead. Deny it
Do I deny God? Do you think I'm just going deny
something because you want me to
It's not about me. She owns you, Adam, but I guess
God does too so there's no point
I own myself
You dream about her
God, you personify cliché
Clichés exist for a reason
Why are you so jealous? I can't recreate the past, and

even if I could, believe me Eve, if could
rewrite the past, if our love was a story,
there wouldn't be a Lilith. I would
erase her from the text. No, I would
never have even written her down
But you would do that to avoid pain, to avoid the
hurt that I feel just so that I would stop
fighting with you. You don't understand
what this feels like
Darling, of course I do. I was jealous once

Back before she left, Lilith planted a garden full of the
most perfect flowers. I didn't name them
until after she left.
How can I possibly compete with the ideal memory
of a wrecked relationship?

THE THIRD NIGHT ALONE

I didn't love her too much, nor did I not love her enough.
I simply didn't love her at all.

My epiphany arrived too late,
In the wrong packaging,
Without enough postage.

— CLASSIFICATIONS —

GENUS & SPECIES: Camassia scilloides
(more popularly known as Wild Hyacinth)

FAMILY: Liliaceae

SOME COMMON TRAITS: Considerable variation in flower color, from typical pale lilac to pale blue

Bulbs tunicated and leaves basal

Abundant in both hill prairies and railroad prairies

It is interesting that Linneus placed hyacinths in the same family as lilies, as genetically, they are quite different, and they are physically more similar to irises, which belong to the Iridaceae family.

I tried to sleep   but the leaves wouldn't keep me warm
                    but the leaves were too hot on my skin
                    but the leaves still smelled of her
                    but the leaves weren't her

Frustrated
I sat up and there was a great burning on my side
Fresh blood moistened the earth
She dipped her white toe in it
Giggled girlishly
And washed my feet with her tears.

But she wasn't Lilith. I cursed God. He waited for me to
hollow my thoughts and replied, I call her Woman. You
name her Eve.

That day, I met   Woman
                    Wife
                    Lover
                    Saint
                    Flawed
And yet, she was still not Lilith

I plunged my fingers into the moist ground to extract God's most perfect creation. The green stem nourished a delicately white bud. I had never seen a color so pure. A drop of fresh rain slid along its slender curves, and through that reflective water, I saw every shade of the world.

DESIRE

I rushed the flower to Adam, eager to please him. Surely, if he could not understand my love for opera, or my appreciation of art, perhaps he could find something in this flower.

I thirsted for beauty. I desired more than man. Adam was not enough.

Why does he reach for the impossible

CROSSROAD

when his fingers can wrap

around this one moment?

Δ

PARABOLA   210

GENUS & SPECIES: Hemerocallis fulva
From Greek: Hemera = day
+ Kallos = beauty

FAMILY: Liliaceae

SOME COMMON TRAITS: Monocotyledons & mostly clump forming

Leaves are strap-shaped, smooth to finely ribbed

Buds small and round at first, then elongating until its maximum length is reached.

It will then Bloom.

Linneus was incorrect to put these daylilies into the Liliaceae family. Modern day DNA analysis has shown that they are more closely related to phormium, putting them in the Phormiaceae family and the Asparagle order.

The past
is a flawless story

                    Distorted

The present
claims her future

But it is a perpetual reminder
of what she has left   behind

CROSSROAD (REVISED)

How could she reach for the impossible
when her fingers can wrap
around this moment?

Content is not synonymous to bliss
And that blissful love
is not offered
Now.

My flower
slipped
through his fingers
collided
onto the sun-cracked earth
to shatter
my love
for him.

THE ESCAPE

In turn,
my feet
automatically
without thought
walked
towards the edge of
his Garden

God calls me Woman. Adam named me Eve.
We have been matrimonially united
Yet she divides the contract of
our unconditional love
Sometimes I can try
to forget that
she was
first
POWER
But
I know
that my love
can overpower
this miniscule memory
that dominates his every thought
I was made from him and to him I will return.
God calls me Woman. Adam named me Eve. I am powerful.

Accustomed to the gentleness of the soft layer of earth
    in the garden
My feet burned on blackened asphalt glazed
    by the brazen sun

FIRST STEP OF KNOWLEDGE

I looked down

                suddenly aware of my nakedness
I was not   ashamed
I was   Cold

The whiteness slowly dissolved
    into technicolored patches.
Her legacy was   evolving
        changing
        morphing
            into something less perfect.

And yet, their flaws made them more beautiful.

COLORATION

I began to obsess over every changing detail. Her flowers were evolving inside my garden just as she was outside the garden. That day, I began to catalogue every lily in the garden, giving everything a distinct and unique name. That day, I fulfilled God's task for me; I became the namer of things.

GENUS & SPECIES: Lilium michiganese
(more popularly called Turk's-cap Lily)

FAMILY: Liliaceae

SOME COMMON TRAITS: Yellow bulbs

Stem nearly 2 m tall, often shorter, glabrous

Some or all leaves whorled, lanceolate, roughened along veins and margins

Flowers nodding

If ingested, bodily reactions may occur, such as dizziness, fainting, or hallucination

Dear Adam,

I've missed you.
I think about you.
About us.
Often.
Do you still tend my garden?

How are the flowers I left behind?
Knowledge is bliss.
Come with me.
Come to me.

I love you.
Still.

Lilith

How could I respond?

I can still taste
the salt
of
her
kiss MYTH

I was wrong

She was not a myth
I can still
feel her skin.

Love is the only myth
I have ever known.

Δ Adam ÷ Δ Eve = inevitable knowledge

Eve, are you still awake
        I'm always awake
What do you think is out there
        Out where
Beyond our garden

CONVERSATION #138

Adam, you used to be satisfied. What's changed

Adam, please answer me

Adam, please

Those odious flowers
Offending olfactory nerves
persevering
to remind him of Her

LILIES

I weed my garden
Thousands of stained lilies
decompose
to appease
my greatest allergy

— CLASSIFICATIONS —

GENUS & SPECIES: Lilium superbum
(more popularly known as Superb Lily)

FAMILY: Liliaceae

SOME COMMON TRAITS: White bulbs

Without auxillary bulblets

Perianth parts strongly recurved, orange-red or orange, spotted with dark purple

Nectar in stem poisonous, particularly if ingested

Do you think the world is any bigger than this
God, Adam, please stop this! Stop talking this way!
Please

I was never content, I want you to know, I just learned
how to cope
You're full of shit. You were content with her
That was a different world. A different Eden
Was it better than this one
Different. Simpler perhaps. We've evolved

CONVERSATION #435

Why can't I compete with her
You're flawless
But I can't satisfy you
She's nothing compared to you. Baby, in a competition for
me, you'd win for sure. She can't compete
against you
Of course she can't. There exists no competition.
She's already won

I don't want to talk anymore. I don't even want to know
what you're thinking

Under her breath, she whispered, I don't want to know. I could hear her, but I ignored what I was not meant to hear. The intense pain in my side would not go away.

FRUSTRATION

Frustrated,
I climbed the exterior wall
Missing a step
I fell
To bruise
My missing rib.

The day Adam fell
God showed His vengance on us.
He blew away everything.

Our shelter was destroyed
Our sun never rose
Our moon bled maroon
Our food evaporated
Only One tree stood strong

—CLASSIFICATIONS—

GENUS & SPECIES: Ornithoglaum umbellatum (more popularly known as Star-of-Bethlehem)

FAMILY: Liliaceae

SOME COMMON TRAITS: Broad green stripe along back side

Rhizomatous plants with a rosette of basal leaves and fewer leaves on the scape

Perianth parts spreading, broadly lanceolate, acute

Used as aphrodisiac in Eastern traditions

Lilith —

Indeed it has been long.
My mind was sickened, but now it is clear. I know what
to do.

If I see you again, it would be pleasant.
If it would be pleasant, I would want to prolong the
experience.
If I would want to prolong the experience, I would be
subjected to love.
If I were subjected to love, I would fall in love with you
again.
This scenario, however, is highly improbable.

RESPONSE TO LETTER #5, RESPONSE #1

It would be nearly impossible for me to fall in love with a
person in the future, if I were still in love
with her in the present. You may interpret
this as it suits you best.

Devoted.
Adam

I used the palm of my foot to crush the flower she left
                                                    behind
It alone had remained white
The other imitations have changed over the years
I looked down
Its purity was branded by the dirt from my sinned toes

SELF-PITY

I ran outside
Ingested one   flower
                 for every day that
Lilith and I had been seperated

A door appeared before me
I opened it
Stepped outside
And realized that I was unclothed

she stands
              between
lost   losing
the past
is a flawed story
                    distorted
the present
can lead to her future   with
                    without   Adam
there is a perpetual reminder
of what she has lost   (the emptiness
               in the garden
             is) too much

why does she reach for the impossible
when his fingers can wrap
around this one moment
promising her discontent?
(dis)content is not synonymous to bliss and that blissful
                    love is not offered Now.
her hungry fingers wrap
around that forbidden   fruit
she smiles & takes a big bite

CROSSROAD (REVISED REVISION)

The point of intersection between the leaves, flowers, and roots is called the crown. It has been said that if it becomes damaged, part or all of the plant will die. If the

lily is ripped from its natural habitat, it will most surely die. The best way to remove it would be to carefully cut it diagonally at a healthy point on the stem.

You awake
  I'm always awake
Did you really miss me while I was gone

  Of course I did
You know, I love you
  Of course you do. I never doubted it.

CONVERSATION #15033

There are 4 phases to the moon: crescent, waxing, full, & waning. 4 is the organizer of time.

There are 4 cardinal points: North, East, South, & West. 4 is the maker of direction.

There are 4 elements: earth, fire, water, & air. 4 is this planet.

There are 4 types of weather: hot, cold, dry, & humid. 4 controls our world.

Perhaps there is more of 4 in Nature than 3.

chapter

4

a father,
a daughter

4

He rubs his hands slowly, not to soften or dull the pain, but to tell skin to start feeling again. He's been trying to convince his hands for over a year now. They don't respond. There must be some language barrier, maybe a mistranslation or a tongue too tonal. His hands in their numbness can't reply, and he rubs his hands so slowly, remembering the time when those same hands were his art.

This is a father, subconsciously lathering skin on skin, each part equally dry, trying to seem strong for a daughter, who notices, often stares at the motion, but tries to pretend that things are as they were before, as she wants them to be.

This is a daughter like any other daughter. She's grown up but still lets her parents call her baby. She's older but she'd still contort herself into impossible pretzels just to get a smile from her father. She would sacrifice more, but she's got nothing left but her body. She would continue to lie, but she's misplaced so many older lies and gets tangled in her own creations. So she watches silently, occasionally looking up to see the repetitive motion of hands frantically searching.

There is a mother, a son, another daughter. There is more family dusted around the globe, but this isn't about them. This about a father and a daughter, both trying to feel, both full of answers, both stubborn and shy enough to never ask the question.

Roles

That which is shown and seen. The pressure of expectation derived from family.

A daughter is many things to a father.

He calls her daughter, but it isn't what he calls her that is important. What she is becomes a compilation of what her father has molded in his mind for her. A father is proud of what his daughter has become, even if she isn't at all what he thinks she is. A father thinks in paintings. In the painting of his daughter, she wears earth tones covered by a white physician's coat. She's still short but thinner than she's been since middle school. Behind

a father, a daughter

her, there are pictures of her children and her husband. They are all variations on a father. The husband looks just like a father, only younger and with more black hair. The children look like a daughter when she was a girl. Every picture is framed in deep mahogany, a wood that he's always loved.

A daughter isn't a physician. She's not even a doctor. She isn't married and doesn't have children. If a daughter gets married, her husband won't look like her father. Her children will resemble her father, but not as he imagines it, but this isn't important. A father always ignores the disconnection between real and irreal. It is what a father does.

A father becomes many things to a daughter. She calls him father, but it isn't what she calls him that is important. What he is becomes a compilation of what his daughter has molded in her mind for him. A daughter is proud of her father, no matter what he is, but she'll never abandon the image of him at his strongest, when she was too young to notice flaws. In this memory, his hair is highlighted with tones of fading black, his belly is large, as if there were a small watermelon shoved beneath the first layer of flesh. He works slowly, not out of necessity but out of leisure. The color of his pupils tells her that he loves her most, more than every one else in the family, more than himself, and everything he does is a sacrifice for her. In this memory, there are no expectations of greatness. There is only a simple happiness without words, a language that refuses to be translated.

A daughter's image of her father is trapped in the past. A father's image of his daughter is a prayer for the future.

A title printed onto blood.

Label

There are many times when a daughter would prefer not to be a daughter, to be someone outside, looking through a stained glass window, everyone inside a different shade of beautiful, someone defying expectation, but she knows she can't escape her label, her daughterness. She will always be a daughter, even when her father has passed, his dreams for her will still be pinned on her body, a nametag that can't be modified. The addition of more labels, more titles, more expectations is the most she can hope for.

Once, a daughter said to her father, I hate being your daughter. I wish I wasn't your daughter. She was angry, spiteful, scared. He laughed loudly. The laughter echoed. Then, he said, You can't run away from what you are. She said, You don't know what I am. This wasn't a lie. To a father, a daughter is always innocent, always nascent, never older than his memory, a majestic little creature who can do no wrong.

A father never wants to escape from his label. He's proud, even when his daughter is angry and spiteful. He shines a little brighter when she's scared. With her fear comes his heroism, a prince ever ready to save her from whatever monstrosity she has created. This is not to say that a father is without fear himself. A father is always frightened. He wishes he could hold up a yield sign for his daughter all day long, even when she's asleep. His caution is another name for fear. He would never tell her this though. Instead, a father often seems overprotective and strict.

A daughter, as a child, has a nightmare. She opens her mouth to scream but whimpers instead. It's the only sound she can make with so much fear pumping through her small body. She knows that her father and mother are down the hall but she can't call out for them. She sniffles, beginning to cry, but then she hears heavy footsteps, footsteps that she knows are her father's. Suddenly, she feels strong and unafraid. She knows that her father is strong enough to stop any monster from hurting her. When his shadow forms a tower over her, she can't even remember what made her feel so scared.

A daughter, now that she has grown, has a nightmare. She is visiting her mother and her father. She sleeps in her old room, filled with ghosts of happy days. In her dream, she sees her father walking and he bobbles from side to side.

He looks up at her and calls her name, and before she can respond, he falls down. His eyes are closed, and a daughter is scared. A daughter is so scared that she wakes up. She looks around. Her father isn't there. He and his shadow are asleep downstairs. At this moment, she suddenly realizes that he can't save her anymore. He's no longer her invincible hero. Instead, she's become the hero. Every time she comes home, her physical body placed in her old bed chases away his worries and this small sentiment allows him to sleep without nightmares.

Teeth

Hardened calcium that exposes emotions in various colors.

When a daughter is young, her father must remind her to brush her teeth every night. In the morning, he checks her breath before she goes to school. When a daughter grows older, doctors put braces on her teeth to straighten crooked genetics. Wires poke and prod, and she bites herself to avoid crying. A father notices this and cooks her soup instead of rice.

When a daughter grows even older and starts smoking cigarettes, she brushes her teeth obsessively to erase the smell and stain. She doesn't want her father to be disappointed that she has picked up his addictions.

A daughter holds so many memories of her father in her mouth. The most common memory is her father sitting in his chair with a pipe in his mouth. Quite often, he's reading, sometimes, he's rubbing his feet, but always, in her memories, he's smoking his pipe. The smell of pipe smoke causes a daughter to salivate. A father smokes Captain Black tobacco. He touches nothing else. A mother hates that he smokes but still buys him canisters at a time.

A father brushes his teeth obsessively, but his breath is always bad. Every night, he scrubs for over twenty minutes. He even uses a tongue scraper. He tells his daughter that a person's teeth tell others about his class. She believes him and spends extensive time in front of the mirror, checking for bits of debris.

A father's top right canine has been removed. Now that he is older, he wears a moustache, sometimes a beard, but always a row of vivid white whiskers. He's trained himself to speak so that his top row of teeth doesn't show. A daughter tries to remember if his mouth had moved like that before the extraction, but memory is too convoluted to paint movement.

Movement

The method of displacement of body from one point to another.

It isn't that a father moves slowly that makes a daughter worried. A daughter is worried because her father is a stubborn man, and even though he's sick, he doesn't take care of his body. A daughter is worried because she doesn't live with him anymore. A daughter is worried because when he walks, his feet barely lift off the ground and the stroke has killed his equilibrium and he falls down all the time and doesn't tell her and he's on the ground. A daughter is worried because he went on a trip to another country and he fell during a shower and bruised his entire body and couldn't get help. He couldn't leave the house for two weeks. A daughter is worried because he didn't tell her about this until six months later. This is why a daughter is worried. This is what keeps a daughter pacing in the middle of midnight.

A daughter is smothered by a mother and a father. When given the opportunity, she moves away, regretfully but happily. The first time a daughter moves away, she only hops up the highway, a test to her parents. She extends her freedoms to a small flair of rebellion, but her father shakes his head, and she returns home. She's scared she might disappoint him. A daughter returns home to remain her father angel: perfect, silent, stagnant.

A daughter can't tolerate perfection so the next time she leaves, she puts states between herself and her parents. It's the only way. A daughter hopes her father can sympathize, but she knows that every choice will only bring more disappointment, and she can't take disappointment so she pretends it isn't there. Sometimes, a daughter thinks

a father, a daughter

that there is nothing worse than the sight of her father shaking his head.

Movement

The method of displacement of body from one point to another.

When a father stands up now, it's difficult. Based on medications ingested, he could be dizzy or sweating, often both, his blood sugar could be too high or too low, his blood pressure could be too high or too low, he could be shaking. This is not a father's natural state. It's the reaction of one pill used to calm the effects of another pill, that was supposed to neutralize his blood sugar but since he didn't eat within half an hour of taking it, it's caused his body to think that his heart has stopped again. And he falls down.

A father sleeps downstairs when he's tired, and he's tired every day. He leaves his wife alone in the cavernous second floor of their home. She dreams of him, moving with ease, of their children coming home to live with them again, of life, a simple pleasure. A father sleeping downstairs doesn't know what his wife is dreaming about, but he's dreaming about the same things. He's hoping that his children will move back to this place that he's built for them, that his wife will be healthy again, that her cancer will stay away this time, that she won't need to cry after shitting twenty times because of some meal dined out, that his life will have been worth all his sacrifices. But really, a father wants happiness for his family, which he can't give them, because by now, he's no longer in control of anything at all.

When a daughter visits home, she feels uneasy. Her father moves slowly, almost limping, and her mother rapidly shuffles to the bathroom after dinner. She's been in remission for the last year, but her colon refuses to be kind to her.

A daughter, sitting in the kitchen with her father, sips at her coffee. A father asks if it's too strong. She says, No, it's perfect. He says, Are you sure? That's strong coffee. It's as strong as the coffee I drink. She says, No, it's perfect. I love it. A father smiles

his
wide
smile. He   thinks
that she's just   like him.
A daughter averts   her gaze to avoid
the gap in his teeth. She wouldn't want to confront all the
implications of a missing tooth. A daughter can't accept that
her parents are decaying.

When a daughter sleeps upstairs, she doesn't think it's so cavernous. When she dreams, she doesn't dream about her family reuniting. She's ashamed that even her dreams oppose her parents.

This is a daughter, hoping her father can sympathize, and this is a father, wishing his daughter could understand. This is a first-generation Vietnamese-American nuclear family.

Humans have 5 senses, and only 5 senses: sight, touch, sound, taste, & smell. 5 is the number of human life and human love.

Jung thought 5 was the number of the natural man. The body and 2 arms and 2 legs makes 5.

Man has 5 virtues and 5 vices.

This is a new age. There are not 4 elements but 5. They are: water, fire, metal, earth, & wood.

Pentagons can never be perfectly aligned. There is always a small space left out.

chapter

news:
(OCTOBER 11, 2005)

5

Today is October eleventh, two thousand five, but the date itself is arbitrary, hardly even important, except that it's important to me, which is to say that it most probably isn't important at all. Today, nonetheless, is a remarkable day because it is indeed the seven month and nine day anniversary of the day that I determined that I would no longer love my darling Turk's cap. It is difficult to visualize that it has been so long. If truth is truth, it has been most trying for me to survive without her, for me to, as they say, allow her to hop out of my reach, but I have managed. I am a strong man, but I feel I must confess that many nights, I do sleep beautiful visions of her.

But certainly that is adequate rambling about my Turk's cap! Today is a new day for me, and because I have endured to rise one more morning, I reward myself by sitting at the New Buffalo Café, and as always, I enjoy a warmed sweet potato muffin brought out by the most perfect of Turk's caps, not that there exist many other Turk's caps, with the exception of course of the real flowers with the name Turk's cap. My dear Turk's cap flutters around the café, and she is a lovely I haven't seen before.

Now I am sure that this scene here appears to display that I have not changed my behavior, but if truth is truth,

there is much that has evolved in my life. I am, even at this precise moment, allowing my love for her to descend. I must confess that I have not been alone in this journey. My physician friend has been most useful. He is kind enough of a man to allow me to spend an extended amount of time with on a regular basis. You see, he has been my, how to say, mentor. You see, my physician friend, when I informed him of my firm desire to stop desiring my precious Turk's cap, wisely suggested that I acquire a habit.

He said to me, My friend, what you need is a distraction! The best way to change a habit is by replacing

news: october 11, 2005

it. This little waitress is a habit, such as smoking, and you need to occupy yourself with something new and invigorating, and that will erase her from your mind.

It is certain that there was luck standing behind me because as he spoke those words, I looked down and found in my lap the Science Times section of *The New York Times*. Now I am not a man who subscribes to belief in black magic, but I should not fail to mention that I am also not a man that lacks an active mind, and if truth is truth, I decided at that very second that I would dedicate all of my time to studying rare and life-threatening diseases. It was, as they say, my calling. You see, there are multifarious diseases in this world, so many in fact that many of these ailments are written on top of, by which I mean, they are forgotten. My physician friend has also assisted me in my poor habit of speaking, as he says. He is quite certain that I speak in an odd manner, and he's been most obliging in correcting all of my, as they say, verbal nuances.

Oh how quickly I am led off path. You see, I believe I was informing you about my new habit, and I am quite positive that you doubt my capacities to simply begin studying diseases. You see, my love for my darling Turk's cap had in many ways made me ignorant of my past. Being as enraptured with her as I was, I was unable to recall a life before her. Of course, now that I am cured of her, I am capable of regaining glimpses of a time without the most perfect of Turk's caps. If truth is truth, I feel that I must confess that before I met my Turk's cap, I was indeed a successful man. Surely, I received a massive sum of money from my family's fortunate death, but also, I had completed my degree as a medical doctor and was in the process of completing my dissertation on the molecular structure of Level IV retroviruses and their inoculum for my doctorate. Of course when my family was killed that most terrible of methods, I found it impossible to complete my studies. If my memory is not flawed, it was the very day that I learned my parents and siblings were dead that I, in my intense distress, on pure accident, stumbled into the New Buffalo Café. This is all such tedious speech though, and if truth is truth, I am certain that I was impassioned about these things in years past, but today I use this knowledge as a method of surviving in a world without my darling Turk's

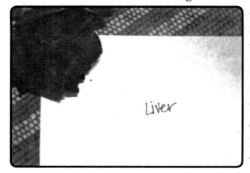

Liver

cap. It has been overtly challenging, but I have been, with my physician friend's assistance over the last seven months and nine days, been steadily extracting the overbearing love I stored for my sweet Turk's cap from my liver[1].

As my liver is cleansed, my history clarifies itself to me, although I am most certain that nothing will be clean in my mind after my Turk's cap has devastated it so.

But as I was saying, I recently visited my physician friend at his office, which although I did indeed promise myself that I would not do again, I had a sore tooth. I am a not an odd man, but if truth is truth, I must admit that I love my teeth, and I was most distressed when a tooth hurt

because I have had since I was a small boy a fear that I would need to have a tooth extracted, particularly one of my canines. I was greatly relieved when he informed

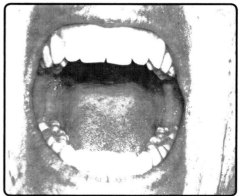

---

[1] It is quite possible that the liver is one of the most popular organs, but very few people know about the rare genetic disease *Ubridio Sukoti-Pneamenon*. People afflicted with this disease have a hybrid liver-lung. *Ubridio Sukoti-Pneamenon* was first found in 1989. If truth is truth, then I must confess that in 1989, I was performing surgery on a premature baby who couldn't breathe on his own. Suffice to admit that when I saw this liver-lung, I silently prayed that the baby would die so I could preserve this amazing anomaly.

me that I had a minor case of gum disease[2], or Gingivitis, which I didn't think was too large of a predicament. My doctor friend, when I laughed, said, My dear friend, oral hygiene is a most serious issue, to which I replied, Come now! At least it was not Gum Disease!, to which we both, as they say, giggled girlishly.

But alas! I've strayed from topic again! What was I saying? Oh yes, my doctor friend, he said to me, My friend, you need a habit that will take your mind away from this girl, and I, in my grand misery, believed that he was correct in his prescription. You see, if truth is truth, I see nothing improper about my small infatuation with my darling Turk's cap. She is a grown woman and very lovely indeed. She is kind, although it is only seldom that she speaks with me, although if truth is truth, it is only seldom that I have the courage to exchange with her as well. Even now, on my seven month and nine day anniversary of the day I determined to stop loving her, I can hardly make noise release from my mouth. Hers is a powerful ability. I must confess that it is that power she has that causes me to return to the New Buffalo Café day after day, and although I certainly do not love her any more, she is irresistible to look upon. Of course, if truth is truth, I must confess that I have always had a, how to say, fear of women. You see, it is true that even if I did not love my darling Turk's cap, which in truth I do not, it would not matter because if either

---

[2] Gum disease is a terribly problematic term, as there are two different instances of "gum disease." The first is the more well known: the oral disease Gingivitis. Lesser known, but more certainly the more fatal, is *Basanismeni Aspheneia Sarkas*. This "gum disease" is a rare disease that is caused by bodily contact with the unrefined, sticky nectar or "gum" of *Ornithoglaum Umbellatus*, more commonly known as the Star-Of-Bethlehem. Like most flowers in the Liliaceae family, this flower itself is not poisonous, but if the bud has been violently ripped from the stem, a fatal nectar is released, and on contact with the epidermis, the venom immediately infects the body. There are, to date, no surviving victims. I must confess that this was my favorite disease to study because if the flower had been cut at a healthy point in the stem at a diagonal angle, the poison wouldn't be released, which is to say that the plant acts defensively and its defenses are powerful. If truth is truth, I have seen only two cases of this Gum Disease, but they were both quite terrible.

scenario be truth, I still would not have the capability to speak with her.

I suppose I have always had this fear of women. My progenitors trained me to fear all those of the opposite sex as they were, as they say, the dangerous pandemic. In retrospect, it was not unwise of them, although their methods were most certainly strangely severe. My father, being one of the forefathers of computers, but never receiving due credit or even payment for it, designed a game[3] on the computer monitor for me. The game's purpose was to visualize how simple it was to impregnate a female. Indeed,

 as a boy, I was aghast! Although the game itself was pleasurable to play, especially because at the time most small children did not have such amazing and, as they say, mechanically sophisticated toys, I was more than appeased with my game. The effect of this playing was quite traumatic for me. I am

---

[3] *Spratos koris Oura* is a disorder that appears in thereabouts 3% of the male population in the United States. Due to the genetic mutation during the late-second trimester, usually caused by some strange bodily ingestion, generally a genetically modified organism to which she is allergic, by the mother, if the being inside her body is male, approximately three-quarters of the tails of his sperm will fall off. Of course, this does not happen inside her body. Somewhere between his twenty-fifth and fortieth year, the boy, now man, will have an instance of ejaculation where, as they say, all of the fallen off tails will dispel themselves from his body. Although men have an endless supply of sperm, the possibility of procreation is greatly reduced. I should mention that the sperm that do remain are severely deformed, and often, the male will be unable to properly ejaculate with orgasm, although his ability to orgasm is not affected. Research pertaining to the female reaction to this bodily ingestion is, as of yet, inconclusive. There is no cure for this disorder. Because of its rarity, I have seen only a handful of men with this disorder, and I must, as they say, divulge that it was not a beautiful vision. I could, of course, only suggest that the men adopt rather than attempt to make babies with their mutant sperm, if you do pardon my vulgarity.

still fearful that I could easily impregnate a woman, and it is not rare that I have nightmares that display a very pregnant Turk's cap. I would never want her to have such a terrible fate. I suppose I should mention that every time I lost the game, by losing I mean that one of the eggs caught the sperm, my mother would force me to wear the burden of baby around my waist. She would then hit my stomach with great strength to inform me of the pains of labor. Then, she would tell me terror tales about pregnancy.

The one I remember most clearly deals with penguins. My mother repeatedly told me stories about penguins that lived in Alaska. Of course, I now know that the Emperor Penguin does not live in Alaska at all, but that piece of knowledge does not change the impact of the story on my nascent developmental ideas of sexual intercourse.

This is the story that I remember:

Penguins are much like humans. They live in groups and have friends. Every year, all of the adult penguins gorge themselves all year long to prepare for a journey. After they are all sufficiently, as they say, overweight, the penguins begin to walk across the great land of ice. Alaska, I was  told, was made of solid ice and there was no soil anywhere. Obviously, today I know that this is not true, but at the time, I was convinced of my mother's accurate knowledge of the way the world rotates.

In any case, the obese penguins waddle across the ice, and when they are tired, they slide on their bellies. This image, of course, still makes me grin, even though I know that penguins do not travel in such a manner. Still, these penguins[4] would venture for hundreds of miles to get to their designated mating ground, and they ate so much before that they can go a couple months without food while they mate and breed. Oh just the idea of this frightens me! There are times when I think about the horror my mother pressured me to endure, and I must pressure myself not to, as they say, think damaging thoughts of the dead. I cannot quite explain why this story has always affected me in such a terrible way. Still, it does not matter as my mother should have been able to tell that I was severely scarred by this story, and she should have ceased torturing me, but alas, she did not, and now, I must reconcile this entire affair on my own.

I believe it was the fear my mother drove in my body that catalyzed my desire to study diseases, and it was a side-affect of my mother seen through the lens of my darling Turk's cap that has caused my recently rediscovered desire to study illness. Of course, I most certainly still maintain other hobbies, such as sitting at the New Buffalo Café and reading *The New York Times* and reproducing some of its most perfect photographs, but my evening hours are spent wearing a white physician's coat sitting near a microscope. If truth is truth, I must confess that it has been difficult to rejoin the ranks of research as I have been quite removed

---

[4] Although penguins are traditionally thought of "cute" or "cuddly" creatures, most people are unaware of the injurious *Puretos Kruos-Poulion*, more popularly known as the Penguin Fever. Penguin Fever is a bodily manifestation of Postpartum Depression. As the new mother experiences the physical disconnection between herself and her baby, her body reacts by shutting down all defensive walls, as I've heard it explained it once or twice. The depression compounded with the body's helplessness actually creates an illness, even if there is no tangible virus, if viruses could ever truly be called tangible. Unlike most viral or bacterial illnesses, Penguin Fever causes new mothers to imagine that their babies have disappeared. Many women claim to see a woman dressed in black take away their babies in a baby bag, which is a bag filled with newborn infants. It should be mentioned that of the women who claim this, 85% of the babies are declared "missing," although it is generally assumed that the mother, in her Postpartum Depression, has killed and eaten her own child. Because there has been so little research invested in this disease, it is hard to decipher whether this is strictly a psychological disorder or if there is some internal viral cause as well.

from the world of illness, except for my own illness of course.

I suppose that some clarification is necessary at this moment. You see, there was a time, seven months and nine days previous to this very day, in fact, that I would spend hours upon hours sitting at the New Buffalo Café, reading *The New York Times*, and watching my darling waitress. There was a time when I would spend extensive time simply staring at her, and I suppose that I could have made her feel uncomfortable, but still, I should mention that she does indeed still call me Herr Doktor, which has been her pleasant pet name for me for the past year. It could most certainly be said, as the saying goes, that her sweet name for me catalyzed my love for her.

Indeed, my physician-friend has told me repeatedly that my darling Turk's cap is not the right woman for me, which is something that I have, as they say, been internally brawling. It is that I cannot stop having small dreams of her. Even though I have, seven months and nine days ago, decided that I could never love her, it has been tremendously restraining to allow myself only two hours of sitting and reading at the New Buffalo Café, rather than my previous habit of spending the entire day here. It is was quite fortunate for my that my physician-friend next gave me the enjoyable prescription of attaining, as they say, a habit, which I have done and with which I grow increasingly enamored.

I should clarify that being that I am terrible with time, I suppose that I cannot even decipher what happened when. Please understand that I am recovering from the terrible disease of infatuation. Even today, today that is the seven month and nine day anniversary of the day that I promised myself that I would stop loving my most precious Turk's cap, I am terribly ashamed to say that I don't think that I have managed to stop loving her and that this entire time has been a lie. I am so terribly frightened that my physician friend will not be able to look at me because I have let him down, as they say, in such a magnified manner. I fear that he thinks of me, as they say, as a dirty pig[5]. I wonder if he even thinks of me as a friend or a patient or if I am merely a piece of bacon to him! Oh this is tortuous! Oh and what if my Turk's cap thought of me the same way? How terrible would it be if she looked at me and thought that I had the mind of a hog? I would make myself sleep in, as they say, mud every night if this could be true. Oh! How could they possibly think this?

No, no. I must calm myself. I know that no one thinks me this terrible, but it is so easy to become excited in terror. When I stop to think about this terrible world and how heartless everyone is, I simply become, as they say, sad. It makes me wonder why I even bother. Most certainly, no one, as they say, cares about anything, much less me and my boring life. I wonder what makes me think my life is interesting enough to even allow myself this time to think. I must certainly attempt to calm down now. I am so upset I wish I could lie down, if only for an hour or two. These thoughts of physicians and pigs, not to even mention my pathetic heart and how it has been, as they say, stomped on by my Turk's cap. It is not fathomable that I have not even, to this day, managed to learn her name. I have walked around for more than seven months and nine days calling her a pet name, and I am most sure that I am certainly infatuated with her, and yet I haven't even the valor, as

---

[5] I have seen many terrible instances of *Megalo Kamogelo Kardion* in my lifetime. It is a most miserable sight! I am, as they say, unsure how to really classify this. It can hardly be called a disease or a disorder. It shouldn't even be call a sickness. Please let me explain. A patient suffering from *Megalo Kamogelo Kardion* has an inflated heart. I am unsure how this starts. Research has shown that the heart begins to inflate due to, as they say, air spheres that become caught in the left ventricle. It is unknown how these bubbles manage this, as the heart, I'm sure you know, functions as an air translator. There is simply no way, as they say, for this to happen. But as I was saying, the air spheres slowly grow in size, which again is physically and biologically quite strange and seemingly impossible. Please do believe me that I do not believe these "studies" as they make no logic to me. But as I was saying, as the bubbles grow, so does the heart until it is so large that the left ventricle and the right ventricle begin to curve upright, making it seem like the heart is, literally, smiling. There is a less than 5% survival rate. I am more than pleased, as they say, that I have helped a woman with this strange occurrence live.

they say, to inquire of her proper name. What a fool I can be.

And yet, now that I am calm, I must verbalize that I cannot be at fault for this situation! This is all because my mother told me those wretched penguin stories as a small male. I remember another tale of a penguin that lived in a neighborhood. The very memory of this nightmarish tale, as they say, makes me perspire. As I was trying to explain, this penguin did not have other penguins to live with him, but he, as they say, was not lonely. Instead, he lived in a community of humans that took very good care of him, as he was not a human but a penguin. There was one family who took particularly good care of him. They

lived next door; however, one day, the penguin caught some sort of fever and was, as they say, bedridden. The family that took care of him could not come over to care for him because they had just birthed a baby of their own, and the penguin, as they say, spent his sickness in solitude. Oh the terror! I don't believe there is a manner to accurately transfer my fear of this story.

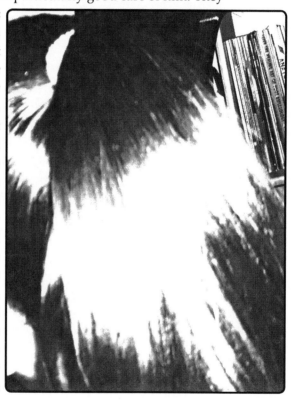

Oh! I am so terrible at maintaining my composure if only to complete one thought! I'm not entirely aware of how, as they say, the subject mutated into penguins, as I am quite sure that I was trying to explain how not even a bull or a bronco[6], by which I mean the wildest of ponies, could disrupt my love for my precious Turk's cap. Often, I have spent extensive time imagining what it would be like to, as they say, not be able to love her, but I cannot bear the image of even a day without her.

I must admit, to my own dismay, that I have, as they say, seen the object of my grimiest desires at least five days out of six days for at least the last year, and although I had indeed promised myself that I would stop loving her, I have not managed to do so. This being the situation, as they say, I wonder if I shall ever produce enough power to leave her. It is a great fear of mine that never will I be free of her hypnotic coffee pouring. Please understand, when I determined seven months and nine days ago to stop loving her, I had every intention of fulfilling my promise, but you must understand that her ways are, as they say, powerful. It is as though every morning, I wake up with only the silhouette of my Turk's cap in my mind. With such an image, it is absolutely impossible for me to go even thirty minutes without seeing her, and most certainly, she does not work every day, which makes my desire to see her immediately multiply fivefold. I fear that it may take some drastic measure for me to stop loving her.

Most certainly, I have told my physician-friend about my most tortuous fears. He has assured me that I should

---

[6] The final patient I ever treated was a woman who became quite severally infected with *Laktisma Alogon*. She was a member of a traveling circus and was accidentally bitten by a young bronco. Now most certainly, I was shocked to hear of circuses employing horses in such a terrible manner, but I, as they say, had more serious issues on my feet. I should, of course, mention that this woman was bitten over a month before she appeared to me for a general physical. It was only during this routine procedure that I noticed that with the slightest provocation, her elbow would jerk backwards, almost as though it was kicking like the wild horse. I was so shocked by this that I began laughing, as they say, like a crazy woman. Indeed, the woman did not find my reaction funny. Despite my original reaction, lab tests revealed that this woman was suffering from a rather severe case of *Laktisma Alogon*, which caused the elbow to fidget. As the infection, as they say, spreads, the entire body will begin to convulse. This will continue for a few months as the poison steadily exits the body. Although painful, there is no alternative but to wait.

not be so concerned, but I am by nature one who is overly concerned about many things. I have, since childhood, been one to care more for strangers than my own parents. Certainly, this could have been in part due to the fact that my parents were quite distant, and they did, of course, die rather early in my life. Such a long period of my life has passed since I have seen my parents that I am increasingly unsure when it was that they stopped living.

My physician-friend, of course, believes that there is absolutely nothing that I have broken, but as they say, I am most certain that if I am to commit to the commitment that I made seven months and nine days ago, I must, indeed move away, and although I am most swiftly becoming comrades with my physician-friend, I cannot withstand the idea of a life without my Turk's cap, nor can I spend more days lurching at Table C5 at the New Buffalo Café.

Alas! I have now wasted hours of my day yet again, and I have had my coffee and my sweet potato muffin, with butter, and I've read the entirety of *The New York Times*, and I believe that I must again come to this conclusion: I must stop loving my Turk's cap. It is impossible that she could ever love me, and without her, my life may as well be as cold and desolate and withdrawn from humanity as

Mongolia's Mountains. It is most certain that mountains are not ideal for survival or even live life, much less my life, but I must do what is correct. I cannot torture my Turk's cap for even one more day. I have read the entire day's news, or at least yesterday's news, and with this knowledge in hand, I am determined to succeed in my small but courageous task.

Today,

October eleventh, two   thousand
five, I will leave the New Buffalo Café, with my *New York
Times*, and I will go bid the loss of my physician-friend, and
I will quickly transport myself to the airport, where I will
purchase one ticket to Mongolia[7], and in Mongolia, I will
once again practice medicine, and my darling Turk's cap
will be free from my suffocating caress of my soft fingers. I
do most certainly fear that she will miss me, but I must be

---

[7] It is popular today to fear the large pandemics that could occur at any moment. Many people fear the Bird Flu or any other number of illnesses that could, as they say, wipe out the whole of man and womankind. I, myself, witnessed a rather large epidemic in 1982 while I was sightseeing in Mongolia's mountains. It is a little known fact that all animals can cry, and in the mountains of Mongolia, I saw the rare *Phonazontas Bouna*, which caused all of the animals residing in the forest to weep. Through the duration of my stay, which in truth was only a week or so as I had an adverse reaction to the food, the animals never stopped crying. When I returned to the States, I was eager to find the catalyst for such a reaction. I found that *Phonazontas Bouna* is a virus that attacks the ENT system, causing an excess of liquid, which can only be expelled through the eyes. Through the years, various incarnations of this virus has appeared in forests, as they say, in all the curves of the globe, but humans have not been infected. Although there is no conclusive evidence to prove this, I believe I saw many animals die of dehydration and sadness.

unfrightened in this. And therefore, I declare that today, October eleventh, two thousand five, I look upon my lovely Turk's cap for the last time.

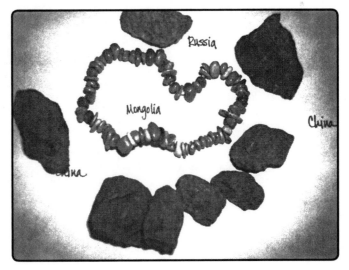

God created the world in only 6 days.

Hrabanus Maurus believed that 6 is not perfect because God created the world in 6 days; rather, God created the world in 6 days because the number itself was perfect.

Jesus's cruxifiction occurred on the 6th day of the week in the 6th hour.

The Star of David portrays unity through the hexagram.

Ironically, chemist Kekule dreamt of a hexagram and from that, he found the molecular structure of a Benzine ring: C_6H_6.

chapter

6

what he saw
(revised)

6

Dark matter covers 95% of what could be the visible night sky. If dark matter covered 95% of the page, this is what we could discern. This is what we could understand. It isn't much.

he saw

a darkness that eats light.
He

cannot exist.

just saw

a vision.

an

evolution

a metaphorical sigh

they saw something

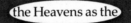

the Heavens as the

merely an optical illusion.

In China, the female has life in stages of 7: a girl gets milk teeth at 7 months and loses them at 7 years; at 14, the road of yin opens with puberty; and at 49 years, she loses her womanhood to menopause.

Also, menstruation occurs for 7 days out of 28.

Also, pregnancy lasts for 7 x 40 days.

Also, the moon changes phases every 7 days.

chapter

7

period:
(a biographical
re-definition)

7

Period 5b. With modifying word: a portion of the career of an artist, writer, etc., characterized by a particular style

He used to wear a lot of black. He also wore variations on black, but mostly, it was black, all black, all the time. He used to sit at the same table every day for hours and read The New York Times. I used to bring him coffee and watch him from behind the counter. For hours, he'd read the paper and he'd cut out photographs and he'd recreate the picture with whatever was handy. It was pretty clever, I thought, substituting salt for a blizzard.

That's the way it was for a long time, maybe a year or more. He'd sit at the same little table and he'd call me his Turk's cap. I didn't know what was Turk's cap is but I liked it. I'd call him Herr Doktor. He looked like a doctor. I wanted him to be a doctor.

For a year, we didn't speak to each other. I offered him coffee, and he watched me work. So that's the beginning. That's how it all began, with him wearing black and me pouring him coffee.

Period 1a. A length of time, esp. one marked by the occurrence of a phenomenon.

To tell his story, I must first tell my own. My name is Period, and for most of my life, I was shy. I didn't speak in public until I'd graduated high school. It wasn't that I couldn't speak. I talked to myself all the time. I don't know, I just couldn't make myself talk to other people. My parents thought I was mute. They took me to all sorts of doctors. The doctors filled my bones with bright colors. Still, I was silent. My mother tells this great fairy tale of how worried they were about me and how they paid specialists and psychologists and everything to come see me and I wouldn't budge, I wouldn't make a single noise, and then one day, she was doing laundry and she walked past my room and she overheard voices. It seems really obvious now, but she opened the door and saw me sitting in my room talking and conversing with myself in full paragraphs, but my parents still thought there was something very wrong with me so they took me to even more specialists who colored my blood with electricy, but I still couldn't speak in public. So I was quiet.

It was kind of the same way him. I mean, we were both quiet for a long time, and then, one of us spoke. One day, he sat at his table and he was recreating a map of Mongolia. I said, Herr Doktor, I hear that in the mountains of Mongolia, there are animals that are afflicted with an incurable disease that causes them to weep until they die of dehydration. I said, Herr Doktor, isn't that the saddest thing you've ever heard?

He said, How did you know that?

I said, It's just what I've heard. Actually, please don't laugh, but I have a fancy for maps. I like to know about landscape and things like that. I like to know what the fauna and flora are in all the different places in the world.

He said, But how did you know about *Phonazontas Bouna*?

I said, What?

I said, Tell me your name.

He said, Period.

I said, Tell me the world.

Period 5d. The interval of time between successive occurrences of the same state or phase in an oscillatory or cyclic phenomenon (e.g. a mechanical vibration, an alternating current, or a variable star)

I want to tell the story of a man. His eyes are crushed velvet, and he is kind. He is a man afraid of everything, and although he loves, he's unable to even speak. I want to tell the story of a man, but I'm afraid it's been told too many times before, and I want to make mine memorable. He is memory, and I need to be authentic.

His name is Period. His parents were astronomers and named him after period-luminosity. They wanted to measure him as they measured the rotation of stars. As a boy, he was most interested in philosophy and religion, but his parents died when he was only five, leaving him scarred. He vowed to never think of religion again.

He lived with his Uncle Adam until he left for college. Adam was a neuropharmacologist. He treated Period, as they say, like his own son. As such, Period had a near normal childhood, playing baseball and soccer, joining the Boy Scouts, going camping. Period was an awkward teenager, partially because his uncle coddled him but partly because he was just an awkward guy. After he graduated high school, he went to college, graduated with honors, and immediately went onto get his M.D. and Ph.D in epidemiology. He never made friends, never had a girlfriend, never went out. Because his only family was his uncle, he rarely even visited home. Period was a serious student, and like many serious students, he stopped caring about what he was studying.

After he received his doctorate, he left medicine and the academy altogether. He began to sit at coffee shops for hours. This is how we met. I poured his coffee, and even though it took him a year to talk to me, I knew he was something sort of spectacular.

> Period 2. The time during which something runs its course, duration; allotted times; natural lifespan.

It was the first day we met. He was crying. His eyes were bloated. He used his large hands to cover his face, ashamed. I said, Can I get you a cup of coffee? He said, Marry me. I said, Of course.

He came in wearing a suit. He was dashing something amazing, and I thought he was some celebrity. I said, Can I get you a cup of coffee? He nodded his head rapidly. He stared at me. I don't even know how long he sat there staring at me, not saying anything, just watching. A year later, he'd finally built up enough courage to ask my name. I said, Period. He said, That's the most beautiful name I've ever heard. I said, My parents named me after a punctuation mark. How's that beautiful? He said, You're beautiful.

It's true that I didn't know his name for a year. It's true that I was infatuated with him and I called him doctor in German. I didn't think he was German. I thought it was funny. I thought maybe it would start conversation. It didn't.

A year later, he still appeared every day and sat at the same table every day and watched me work every day. Finally, I said, Let me buy you this cup of coffee. He said, Maybe I can buy you a cup of coffee? He said, What's your name?

We went to middle school together. He was quiet. So was I. One day, I walked past him and accidentally touched him. He was a firecracker. He said, What's your name?

I sat in the New Buffalo Café reading and he brought me a bagel with hummus, and I said, I didn't order this. He said, You looked hungry, and I wanted an excuse to talk to you. I said, I'm busy. He said, I'll be here when you're done with your busyness. I liked his boldness. I liked his confidence. I said, What's your name? He said, Period.

It's true that I didn't know her name for a year. It's true that I was infatuated with her and I called her a colloquial name for a flower. I didn't think she was a flower, I wasn't confused. I thought it was clever. I thought maybe it would start a conversation. It didn't.

A year later, she still appeared every day and offered me coffee at the same table every day and watched me work every day. Finally, she said, Let me buy you this cup of coffee. I said, Aren't you tired of coffee yet? I said, Let's start with a name.

It doesn't matter how the story begins. Our story has thousands of variations, each one equally interesting, but our story, our real story begins with a name.

> *Period 1b.* The time during which a disease runs its course; the time occupied by each attack of an intermittent fever. Also: each of the successive phases in the progress of a disease.

A name exchange and hours of talking, we must've talked for days. It was as if our silence was a sickness, and now cured, the accumulation of words in the mucus membranes demanded release. We had a hard time listening, we were so eager to hear the sound we could make from our own lips and throat.

> *Period 6.* A major division of geological time; spec. one that is a subdivision of an era and is itself divided into epochs.

Looking at his hand, I said, Your palm is a map. I wonder where I would travel if I followed every line until its end.

He said, Please don't leave me.

I covered his hand in ink and made a print. The sun shined the day I left. I said, I promise to come back. He said, Please don't leave me.

I found dragons at the end of his heart line.

When I returned, he said, The sun hasn't stopped shining since you left. It didn't set at night. All day and all night, the sun beat down on me. I wanted to curse the Solarians for their sadistic humor. Our garden is destroyed. My skin is burnt. I haven't slept. Not even for a minute.

I said, But darling, I found dragons.

Because the sun never dove into the horizon, he began to believe weeks were minutes, days were seconds, each tick long in its tediousness. He would guess I had left him for only a day, a very long and hot day. While I was gone, he lived in a bright vacuum obsolete of time and space. He lived in bright dark matter.

> *Period 7b.* The time in which a celestial object, satellite, etc., performs one revolution about its primary (or about the centre of gravity of its system) or rotates once on its axis.

The café being small and him sitting in the middle, I orbited him. In his seat, he spun complete circles watching me go round.

> *Period 7d.* Any length of time defined by the regular recurrence of a phenomenon or cyclical process.

Every day.

> *Period 13.* The highest point reached in any process or course; a zenith.

I'm not wrong. This isn't all a dream. This happened. I was a waitress and he sat at the café. I asked him his name, no, he asked for mine, but it doesn't matter. Memory confuses, but I loved him and that was real, but now he's gone. He's left and is no more. A disappearance. A death. I'm not sure which. He said, I have to search for dragons. I said, Dragons don't exist. They're made up. They're not real. He said, I have to find the dragons. I said, Please don't leave me. He said, I'll return when I find them, and he did. He came back but he wasn't the same. He was tired. His face looked like leather and he carried with him a burden, and I seeing him return, I was reveling, and he with his sadness and his weight, he couldn't see me I was so high up.

He didn't look for dragons though. I went. I went and I found them, and beyond them I saw a man carrying the weight of expectation on his shoulders, and he was the one that told me that dragons don't exist, and he was the one that told me not to leave. We stood there, on top of a mountain, its peak only broad enough for the two of us to stand, and I don't know where he is. I don't know where Adam went at all.

I want to tell the story of a man, a man I love, but I don't have enough memories, and now I'm afraid that the dragons were never real.

> *Period 4.* An indefinite portion, spell, or interval of time; a portion of one's life.

Once, there was a man named Adam. He wore black because he was sad. He read the newspaper and collected photographs. He drank coffee, black, and I poured it for him. We were shy, the two of us. We both wanted nothing more than to speak, but we couldn't. I can recall all this with surety. Adam, I've loved you for so long. Why can't I remember? He drank his coffee black, and I poured it. I never spilled even a drop. One day, he asked my name, and we didn't stop talking for weeks. I don't know why we stopped, only that we did, only that one of us went searching for something and returned never the same. I know that my name is Period because his name is Period, and when defined, period is the end of something.

> *Period 15.* The end of a journey; a destination.

Buddhists believe in the Eight Fold Path.

There are 8 petals on a lotus flower.

The I Ching has 64 hexagrams. DNA *has 64 codons.*

chapter

8

8

I can't see A, B, or C. I only know that A, B, and C exist. To me, they're just variables. They could be x, y, or z. They're just empty letters meant to signify three people, three anonymous people. If I saw any of them, I wouldn't know it, nor would I know which one of the three they were. But I know their ages: A was 4; B was 5; C was 6. I use the past tense because they're older now. It's been at least five years, but even the time that has elapsed is arbitrary. Even time could be a variable, let's say variable B. Today, I only see these variables and the numbers attached to them, which are supposed to represent the victims and their appropriate ages when they were molested by R, not the same R that molested me, but an R I know all too well.

For purposes of clarity, I will call the R that violated me will be called R_1 and the R that violated A, B, and C will be called R_2.

Names have a tendency to blur details. It's unnecessary to know that R_1 and R_2 don't just have the same letter in their first name. It's superfluous for me to say that they're both named Robert, and even though they share the same first name, they have different patronymics. It would be useless for me to explain their different DNA because there's simply no reason for me to split hairs without reasonable cause.

R_2 sits in a room made of wood. Twelve people are seated to his left. He pretends that he doesn't see their looks of unabashed disgust. These twelve people can't see his wrists. They're covered with pussing welts from his struggle against steel. He has a habit of hiding what he's embarrassed of.

R_1 is full of blubber and waste. Even when he was 13 and I was 9, he was fat. My family puts a lot of emphasis on the body, especially the female body. R_1, being a boy, wasn't exempt from scrutiny, but his fat was funny. Mine will always be seen as disgusting. In my memory, I see fat, thick skin rolling over his belt line, but I know that I didn't really spend time noticing his body then. At 9, I didn't notice anyone's body. I barely even noticed my own. The image that I have of him comes from old pictures and my current idea of him, a physicality tainted by a disgust that refuses to subside. He's even fatter now than before. The few times I've seen him, I've averted my eyes. I'm unsure if I didn't want to see his degeneration or his proliferation.

He doesn't look at the other people in the courtroom. Instead, he strains his brown eyes to unscramble the faces in front of him, making it look like he is crying. R_2 doesn't look guilty. He looks sad and repentant. The twelve disgusted people don't know how to interpret this.

His hair is closely buzzed. His face is still swollen with baby fat. He wears a dusty and old black suit. He looks incredibly young, too young to be in that courtroom, too young to be charged with such disgusting crimes. He's only sixteen. The defense would have you believe that he did not realize the gravity of his actions.

Of course, I wasn't there. I never saw any of it. He's inferred a sentence here and there, but he's never even told me what he did. I can only imagine what R_2 looked like. I found his picture on the Internet, an invasion of privacy that is no longer his privilege. His headshot doesn't look like him now. He's lost weight, grown out his hair. Still, he's marked, and people throw rocks at him when they see him walking down the street, passing their children, running neither towards nor away from him.

When I visit my hometown, R_2 and I sit outside his room. We smoke cigarettes. R_2 keeps one foot inside the house. It's impossible for me to ignore the black chunk of plastic strangling his ankle, a global positioning system that may as well be programmed into his brain. No chances, he says. I can't take any chances this time.

Back then, I didn't know what he'd done. I only knew that he'd done something, something so abhorrent that he wouldn't tell anyone. I was too embarrassed for him to ask. He'd make false references to prostitution, an act of sexual misconduct that I didn't find morally repugnant. Maybe that's why I accepted it so easily.

A few weeks later, I'd built up enough curiosity to look up his name on the sex offenders' web page. I'd known him, worked with him, driven him home, trusted him for more than a year. He hadn't trusted me with this information so I didn't look away. My eyes weren't shaking between the slats of my fingers. His personal web page didn't give me any finite answers, only vague inferences that forced me to build the most horrible story possible.

DE-CONSTRUCTORS: are more esoteric. They would spend more time molding a perfect sphere out of clay than building a skyscraper. They are focused on beauty, but not their own. They often look extremely sloppy and disheveled, but they are never overweight. De-Constructors are extremely conscious of everything they put in their body.

Scenario 1:

The		Man		Pedophile		Monster		Asshole	
Has	x	Touched	+	Molested	+	Destroyed	+	Raped	=
Our		Children		Boys		Babies		Innocence	

Scenario 2:

The		Children		Boys		Babies		Guilty	
Have	x	Imagined	+	Framed	+	Cried	+	Pursued	=
His		Guilt		Lies		Name		Innocence	

Scenario 3:

Neither 1 nor 2 are accurate, but they both tell a certain amount of truth.

Scenario 4:

Three Counts of Aggravated Sexual Assault. Convictions do not lie.

Scenario 5:

In my mind, R_2 can't be a monster. I refuse to believe that he could have taken those small bodies, full of smiles and bubbles, and molded their soft skin into his playground. It just isn't possible.

I don't wonder if I'm wrong, but often, I traipse through all the possible scenarios. Then, I tuck them safely into my socks so that no one else can taste the heinous decay of imagination. When I sit outside with R_2 smoking cigarettes, I don't take off my shoes.

When R_1 is 13, he acquires a girl to hang on his arm. She lets him kiss her, and sometimes, she lets him touch her body. It is apparent that

R

she is quite fond of his body. In a letter, she dotes on him. She says she dreams of the smell of his aftershave. Reading his letter, I laugh because he doesn't shave.

CONSTRUCTORS: are completely focused on money & building. They care so much about social status that they often forget to take care of themselves. Often, Constructors bald very young and have potbellies. They eat fast food and microwave dinners because they don't have time to cook. 88% of Constructors have either colon cancer or a stroke before the age of 62.

Between intervals when R_1 and his girl are not kissing and touching, a warm fear builds in his immature head that he may not know how to properly touch his girl. He worries he may be too soft or too callous, too tender or too rough. It isn't that R_1 is pro-active. R_1 and I are cousins. He says that family should always help out family. He says that's what family's for. He says he would do it for me. He says I'm ungrateful because I play his Nintendo and I play his Sonic Gameboy and I won't even help him out with something small like this even though he lets me play with all his toys. Even his Ninja Turtles. He says I'm a spoiled brat. Then he reasons with me, even though he says I'm an unreasonable little girl. Of course, I believe him.

A, B, and C are not related. They're friends playing in the street. They imagine elaborate fictions with princes and beanstalks and bicycles and mazes. They play games, and C, being the oldest, usually wins. R_2 watches them with his feet folded neatly under his butt. He wishes he could watch children play every day.

I am Donatello, the smart one, but mainly because my favorite color was purple. He is Leonardo, the leader. Even though my second favorite color is red, I don't get to be Raphael. I'm stuck with Michaelangelo, the airhead party animal. Any one who's watched Ninja Turtles knows that Leonardo and Raphael are the ones that really save the day so when R_1 and I play Ninja Turtles, he always wins. He says that he's the winner and the winner should always get a prize. I offer to steal him a cookie from Grandma's secret stash.

DOERS: rarely have time for fun. They're always doing something, and that something is generally useful. That's not to say that they never have fun, but for a Doer, fun has a designated time and space, and if life throws this fun time a lemon, the Doer doesn't make lemonade; he makes lemongrass. Doers are particularly special people because they do more than expected and exceed everyone's expectations. Generally, Doers don't have any friends, partially because no one can stand an ass kisser and partially because Doers can't take enough time out of their immaculately planned days to make or maintain friends. It's a lonely life.

To say that a crime is aggravated only means that is has features that make it a worse act, generally this implies the use of a weapon, although this is not always the case with sex crimes. To say that a crime is aggravated means that the criminal who enacts said crime can be punished by being locked in a cell for a longer amount of time than if the crime is not aggravated. To say that a crime is aggravated only means that the criminal will be locked up, in a cell, with adequate food, water, shelter, and even entertainment. The money that the parents of A, B, and C give to the government every year is used to facilitate this punishment.

ACTIVE: personalities tend to be strong characters. They exude a sense of determination & can be seen as aggressive. An Active personality often resorts to alcohol to calm himself down after such an Active day. He's exhausted and irritable, which is why the slightest provocation can bring about a frenzied rage. During these rages, the Active personality dominates all other personality traits, and the person blocks out all memory of this time. It is not uncommon for unusually violent behavior, mostly rape and other sexual molestations, to be exhibited during this time. They are only trying to actively engage whatever it is that they are currently focusing on. Active personalities tend to try to blaze through tasks. Active personalities have a better understanding of self because they are always trying to improve themselves. They tend to be provocateurs.

If R_1 is 13, then I am 8. If A is 4, B is 5, and C is 6, then R_2 is 16. These numbers don't make a pattern. There isn't a formula to unite them. I want there to be formula, a solution, a connection, but there isn't.

If R_2 is 17 when he is convicted of 3 counts of aggravated sexual assault against a minor and is 21 when he is released, then the amount of time he spent in a juvenile detention center is equivalent to the number of years A had been alive before he was introduced to R_2's sadistic world of sexual fantasy.

I begin having nightmares at age 17. I see terrible images of R_1. Freud would call this repression. I don't tell my family until two years have elapsed since the initial memory struck. I don't know why I refrain from telling them my secret. Freud would also call this repression. My memory isn't full. There are long gaps missing. I try to sew pieces ... hypnotically patching together dreams, ... blotted with blu...

My broken doll with yellow hair blinks from her box. I supposed to be asleep. Mot[her] snores lightly. I hold a clu[mp] of her hair, spiraling it aro[und] my pinky. The doll is aw[ake,] alive, a life. I want to sm[ell] her eyelids. I didn't want [the] doll. I've only ta[lked to its] plastic casing ... It stinks of m... something... somethin...

Fingers travel aimlessly, tirelessly. I close my eyes tightly. His breath is fis[h] full of sweat. I wa[nt to] close my nose, p[ut up a] sign that says, Go A[way] but I know that he cannot [read.] He is illiterate. [H]e tells me that ... that I owe ... [requ]ired a debt ... his toys, ... [neve]r be in ... [n]ickels ... [eno]ugh for cream...

Grandmother calls from the other room. She has fallen on the ground again. Naked, he lifts his body to dress and Pick her up. ... the telepho[ne.] I tell him, I remember what you did to me. You ruined my life. ... beauty, touch, but will ... to smash ... will make ... glue, which I [ca]n use to make mosaics of my nightmares.

I'm unsure what all this means. At night, I sweat and grind my teeth. Awake, I smoke cigarettes, file my nails down with my teeth. My poor teeth are forever damaged. Because of that, I never smile in pictures, even when I was a child. I had no choice. I was embarrassed.

We pl[ay] Mario Bro[thers] Nintendo. He [wants to] be Mario, and [I am] forced to be Lu[igi.] ... that, I prefer tall, ... stout and strong ... what I've been trai[ned] I learned that we h[ave] choices in life.

... me and ... had no choice. ... make a fool out of myself. I have to impress her. You understand, don't you? That's what family is for, to learn and grow.

... illiterate ... me that ... at I owe ... [requ]ired a debt ... [playin]g with his toys, and one must never be in debt. I count saved nickels that are never enough for what I owe.

[inverted text at bottom:]
... can use to a cream... my eyes ... never ha... some... it stink... plastic ... doll. ... her ... alive, a life. The doll ... my pinky. spiraling it arou[nd] hold a clump ... Mother. ...sleep...

I call him on the telephone.

Naked, he to dress She the ...ther

I'm unsure what ...ave. I want, but will ...yes together. I want to smash ...y wad of glue. It will make ...e to make mosaics, which ... mares.

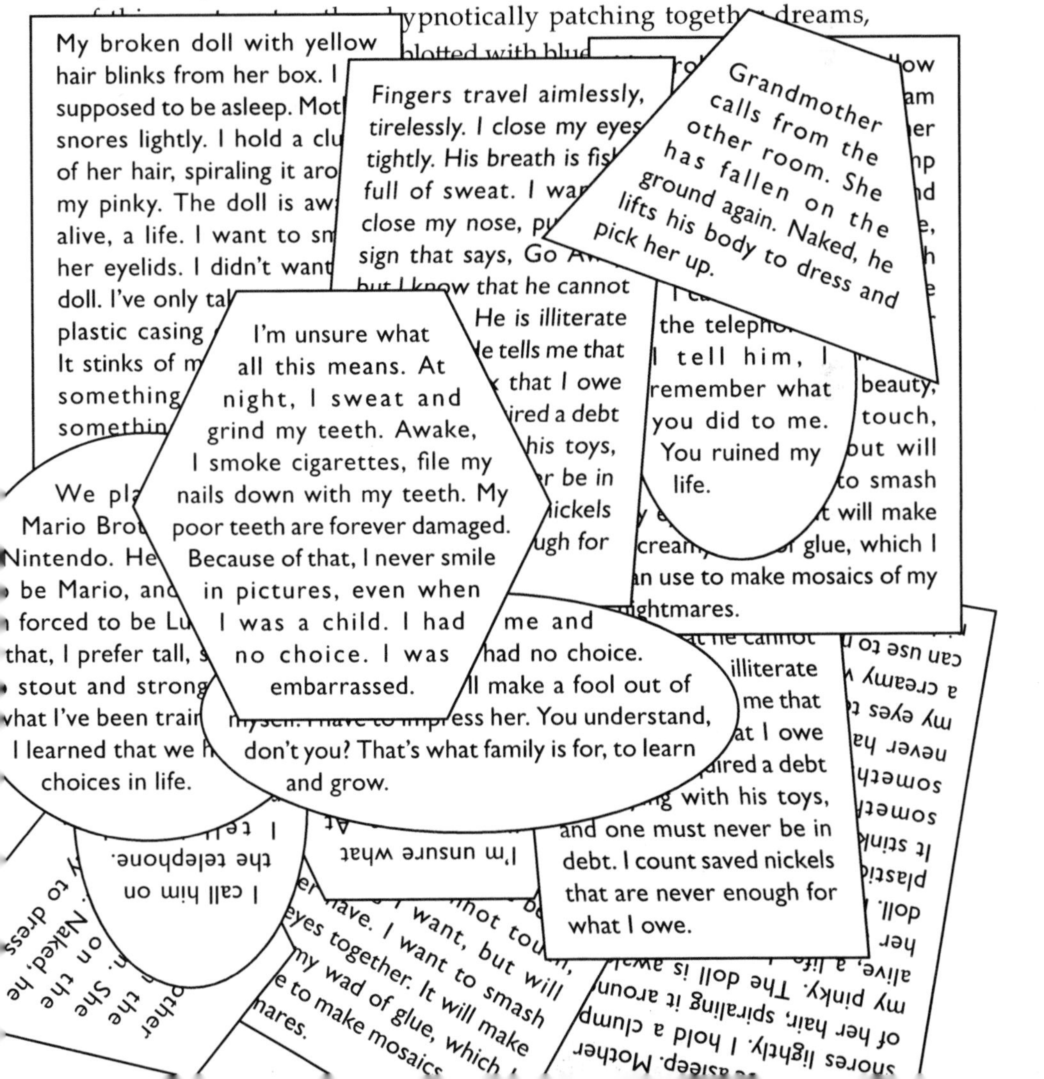

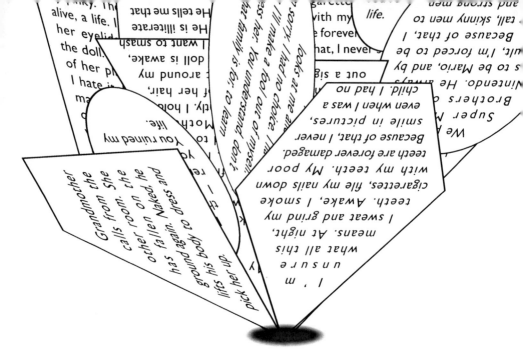

R₂ spends 4 years locked in a cell, with every convenience but physical freedom. He's even allowed to go outside for most of the day, without any restraint but the fences. 4 years for 3 children. Again, formulas and patterns are deficient. R_2 will spend the next ten years on parole and house arrest. The terms of his freed confinement are: weekly meetings with a parole officer, weekly sex offenders' group therapy, bi-weekly counseling sessions, steady employment, no internet, no costumes of any kind that may attract children, his face and crimes posted on the web, and an hour allowance for travel to and from work and meetings.

     If I were to chart the gravity of causes and effects, R_2 would be seen as overtly fortunate, but statistics are much more powerful. The truth is that early release and this kind of quasi-freedom for sex offenders is more common than brown hair and blue eyes.

I attempt to build a home out of my experience with R_1, but the patches are too awkward, some pieces too large, some too ephemeral, some without any purpose at all. I remember things that couldn't have happened, but they've dissolved into my truth. Instead of building a home, I cause fault lines to tremble. I can't stop earthquakes from burrowing rifts in my family.

MASOCHIST: personalities tend to let rational thought dictate action. This is not to say that whatever decision is made will be the most "rational" though. Rather, Masochist personality only means that they prefer to think through scenarios, following every possibility, before acting. Much like the Sadist, the Masochist has also been misunderstood. He is not in any way cold or malicious. In fact, Masochists very much so look for approval. This is why he works so hard to be rational. He doesn't want to appear "soft" and will often hide behind sarcasm to save face.

Now, when I talk to R_2, I want to throw up. His words are empty. He says he met this guy on the bus the other day, and oh god, I'm so embarrassed, and please don't be mad at me, but I made out with him, right there on the bus. And he was the best damned kisser ever, and I've kissed some men in my lifetime, let me tell you.

THINKERS: never shut up. Unlike the Doer though, he never actually gets anything done. All that the Thinker does is talk and talk about whatever it is that he's trying to figure out. Often, Thinkers develop some sort of sleeping dysfunction, whether its sleep talking or violent behavior during the REM stage. These are common warning signs for schizophrenia, which many Thinkers are afflicted with. Thinkers tend to develop this illness because their thoughts are in constant competition with each other, and the Thinker himself is left dumbstruck as to which voice or argument to believe. In general, Thinkers don't live past the age of twenty-six and a half. The most common method of suicide is death by hanging.

He says he's going to be celibate from now on. He says that sex has been the worst thing to ever happen to him. He says he's going to stay away from all men, no matter how much they hit on him. No matter how hot they are. I smile, thinking that no one hits on him. His face looks guilty, but aside from that, it's also shaped like an alien face, like a smooth E.T. His voice is raspy but shrill.

Still, I find myself addicted to his friendship, trying to make a relationship work with another R, to mend what has frayed with R_1, but I can't tailor my cousin. He has too many ripped seams.

SADIST: personalities tend to let emotion dictate action. This is not to say that whatever decision is made will be the most "caring" though. Rather, Sadist personality only means that they prefer to consider the repercussions of their actions on those around them before acting. Because sadism has been given a negative connotation in today's society, it is important for one to understand the positive aspects of the Sadist personality. Sadists tend to be most kind and caring people, much more so than any other personality type.

I don't live in the same city as either R anymore. Even then, R_2 calls me almost daily. He tells me the most mundane details about his day in the most flamboyant way, and I try to pay attention. When I return to the city, I see R_2 as little as possible, but I feel guilty about it. I don't tell him that I know. He doesn't offer any more information. He wants a friend who won't judge him for what he's done. When I return to the city, I don't see R_1, but my family tries to ignore what I've told them, and on accident, we coincide shifts at family gatherings. He's disgusting. His life is a mess, and in some small way, I revel in that.

A, B, and C are cousins. They visit their Uncle Robert. They don't see him often, but they like him all the same. When they leave, they laugh at his squeaky voice. They think he's a goof. They don't cry to their mother or father. They don't want to talk about it so they pretend that it never happened. Uncle Robert has cool games for them to play. He's got the new PS2. It's a new generation, and technology is much better now then when I visited my cousin Robert.

R_1 never sits in a room made of wood. No one will take control of his body like he took control of mine. He will never have people throw rocks at him for what he did. This was my decision. I never take control.

The first family member I tell is my sister. I am eighteen, away from home, depressed, anxious, and cursed with memory. I see a psychologist who tells me to see a psychiatrist who tells me I'm crazy and hands me pieces of paper that represent all of my mental illnesses. I call it genius. They call it bipolar. I hold the pieces of paper in my pocket, secretly proud that now I can join the club of fucked up artists. I call my sister to ask her for money. I only tell her because I don't want my parents to know. I'm Catholic and store guilt more easily than fat. I don't want my parents to be sad. I have no real justifications.

Rightfully, R_1 should be punished in some way.

A, B, and C don't really know each other at all. They've never met. Their parents drop them off at a cheap day care. It's the cheapest they can find. A teenaged boy greets them with a big, fake smile. A, B, and C run off to compare toys. They meet more kids. D, E, F, and G are already inside. They play and eat and nap, and when they nap, R_2 stands over them.

For females, rape is penetration. For males, definitions vary. Bodies can be easily fooled though. Fingers can be as erect as cocks. Fingers can rip flesh as well as any other body part.

I am no longer 18. I don't think that crazy is an elite club, and I no longer subscribe to medical cocktails. My family hopes that in my insanity, I falsely accused R_1 of the most ugly crime. We don't talk about it. I want to vindicate myself. I want to tell them that I didn't make it up. Instead, I hide in tight shirts and a childish voice. I know this. I also know that it wasn't just R_1 that did this to me, even though I want to blame him for everything.

The first time I see R_1 again, I'm nineteen years old. I'm a recently converted feminist, jarringly anti-male, with a shaved head and piercings all over my face. He comes up to me and hugs me. He says, You aren't still mad at me, are you?

I want to punch him, but I don't. I look at him, almost crying, and reply, Of course I'm not. How could I be mad at you?

He's fat and really very ugly.

R_2 calls me crying. He's failed a mandatory polygraph test. He says it was because he was nervous. He failed two questions, even though failure is the wrong word. The questions were: 'Have you had sexual intercourse with anyone from your place of employment since your release?' and 'Have you had sexual intercourse with a minor since your release?' He tells me that it's because he flirts with people at work that his guilty conscience must have had such an impact on him that it registered on the test. He says that he hasn't done anything with anyone at work, my work. The place I've worked for the last 8 years. I want to believe him very badly. He says he swears that he hasn't done anything. It's just friendly flirtation. He says that he hasn't had sex with a minor either. That this one time, he didn't look at a guy's ID, but the guy looked young, really young, and even though he said he was eighteen, he looked young, and that must have been why he failed that question. He says he doesn't want to go back to jail because he isn't a minor anymore, and he'd have to go to real prison. He says that juvy wasn't bad, but prison will be bad, especially for a gay sex offender. He doesn't mention that he was a child rapist. He always manages to leave out that small detail.

Of course, he says the exact same thing to his therapist and his parole officer, and they increase surveillance on him but don't arrest him. He calls me and says how relieved he is but he isn't surprised because he wasn't guilty.

When I'm 14, the school doctor tells me that I need glasses. I'm embarrassed. My sister takes me buy glasses that she thinks are cool, but they're hideous. I refuse to wear them, and by 17, I can barely see writing on a chalkboard if I'm sitting in the front row.

R_1 works at Eye Masters. When I visit him, I don't remember anything. He makes my glasses, and they aren't bad looking. I visit him again at 23. I ignore my accusations, saying that I've forgiven him, but I haven't. He pays for two pairs of glasses and cleaner for me. I think he does this out of guilt. He tells me I should get contacts or laser surgery. He tells me his mom got it done and she sees great. I ask him why he hasn't gotten it. Or contacts for that matter. He tells me he likes his glasses. He says he likes the feel of it on his face.

REACTIVE: personalities do not act until provoked.
They will tend to be the followers and follow directions perfectly. They do not deal well with authority, unless there is someone above them giving them instructions. It

is not that Reactive personalities are submissive. It is just that they prefer to react to situations rather than provoke them. Reactive personalities also tend to carefully complete tasks. Reactive personalities make excellent stalkers and assassins.

I say something nice in response, but I'm disgusted at myself for talking even to him, for being supportive of him, for this.

Christ died in the 9th hour.

Troy was sieged for 9 years. Coincidentally, this is how long Odysseus was lost.

There are 9 muses: Calliope, Clio, Erato, Euterpe, Melpomene, Polyhymnia, Terpsichore, Thalia, & Urania.

Speaking about Beatrice, Dante said that 9 was her true self.

chapter 9

9

: smarts tester
(version 9.9)

9

DEAR TEST-TAKERS:

Thank you for trying out our newest version of the SMARTS TESTER! This is the best Intelligence Quotient indicator available. In fact, we have a 99% satisfaction rate. There's no need to boost the image of this test though.

You're about to experience the most intense, most mind-teasing, most accurate IQ test out there, and we hope you'll LOVE it!

At this time, we'd like to take the chance to go over a few quick instructions.

INSTRUCTIONS:
1. This is a timed test.
2. You have 15 seconds per question.
3. If you don't know the answer to a question, guess.

Enjoy the SMARTS TESTER, Version 9.9.

Sincerely,

A. B. Adams, Ph.D.

SMARTS TESTER, Version 9.9.

SURVEY

Before taking this test, please fill out this brief survey. It will help the test evaluators assess your cumulative intelligence quotient in a more accurate manner.

Surname:

 A. Miss

 B. Mrs.

 C. Ms.

 D. Mr.

 E. Dr.

 F. Esq.

What is the highest degree of formal education you have achieved?

 A. Some high school

 B. High school diploma

 C. Some College

 D. Technical school

 E. College diploma

 F. Graduate school

 G. Medical or Law school

 H. Post-Graduate work

 I. Other please specify _____

In what field do you work? _____

What is your position? _____

What is your income bracket?

 A. less than $10,000

 B. $10,000 - $15,000

 C. $15,000 - $30,000

 D. $30,000 - $50,000

 E. $50,000 - $100,000

 F. more than $100,000

SMARTS TESTER
Version 9.9

1. *Based on the color spectrum, how would these boxes be ordered?*
   - **A.** C, B, A, D
   - **B.** B, C, A, D
   - **C.** D, B, C, A
   - **D.** D, A, B, C

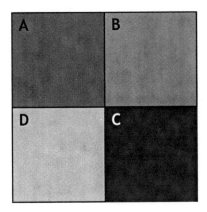

2. *Three geese and five dogs have how many legs?*
   - **A.** 33
   - **B.** 26
   - **C.** 28
   - **D.** 24

3. *Which of the following three numbers, when added together, makes 21?*
   - **A.** 1, 8, 9
   - **B.**
   - **C.** 9, 7, 4
   - **D.** 2, 6, 10

4. Which of the following words can be spelled using only the letters in "ambidextrous"?

    A. score
    B. spade
    C. braid
    D.

5. Which words would appropriately correspond with these numbers: 24, 5, 3, 60?

    A. Hand, Seconds,   , Triangle
    B. Hours, Fingers
    C.   ,   ,   ,
    D.   ,   ,   ,

6. What is the missing letter?

    A. I
    B.
    C. M
    D.

B	A	C
C	B	E
E	C	H
H	E	?

7. *34 minutes before 5 is how many minutes past 4 o'clock?*
   A.
   B. 28
   C.
   D.

8. *If the word "jake" means spicy, which of the following sentences is grammatically correct?*
   A.
   B.
   C. You're such a jake.
   D.

9. *Which of the following words use all the same letters?*
   A. Pretentious
   B.
   C.
   D.

10. *What is the thirty-second letter to appear in this sentence?*
    A.
    B. P
    C.
    D.

11. *By removing seven letters from "fatherhood," what word can be spelled?*
    A.
    B.
    C. hoe
    D.

12. Which comes next in the sequence?

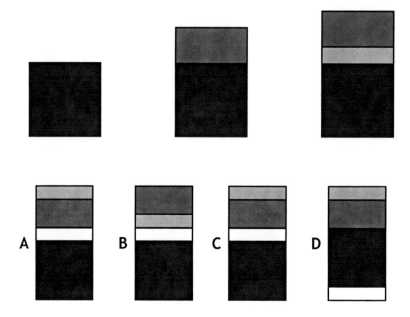

13. Which of the following sentences is palindromic?
A.
B.
C.
D.

14. Which   ?
A. Looking at those eyes now, I find them disgusting,
   but I still want to hold them near.
B. They care about physical appearance
   and social status.
C. There are times when she twirls by and I get a
   glimpse of her thigh, tan and firm.
D. He began to teach calculus at
   the local university.

15. *Holland is bigger than France. Japan is smaller than Holland.*
    Holland is the same size as Australia. The U.S.S.R. is the
    bigger than Japan. Which of the following statements is true?
    A. Maybe he was just dehydrated.
    B. Freud would call this repression.
    C. She has a son and a husband that she can't leave.
    D. Everyone wants to be Dutch.

16. *Mandarin is to Chinese as _____ is to Pakistan.*
    A.
    B.
    C.
    D. Swahili

17. *Which of the following does not belong:*
    Neptune, Mercury, Mars, Pluto, Vulcan?
    A.
    B. Vulcan
    C.
    D.

18. *Pick the answer that best completes the series:*
    Dollar, Franc, Peso, _____.
    A.
    B.
    C.
    D. Money

19. *The sum of all the numbers between 1 and 12*
    is _____.
    A.
    B.
    C. Prime
    D.

20. Which number should come next in this series:
5, 17, 29, 41, ___?
A.
B.
C.
D.

21. Which of the following does not fit?
    A. A
    B. B
    C. C
    D. D

21. Which of the following best completes the sequence?

 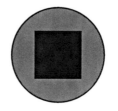 

23. *If the day before yesterday is three days after Saturday, what is today?*
    A. Wednesday
    B. March 02, 2005
    C. Mexican food day
    D. October 11, 2005

24. *Which of the following does not fit: Poodle, Golden retriever, Siamese, Pug?*
    A.
    B
    C.
    D.

25. *If you re-arranged the letters V-T-T-E-R-D-L-U-O-E, you would get a _____.*
    A. Loverutto
    B.
    C.
    D.

26. *Which number should come next in this series: 144, 121, 100, 81, _____?*
    A.
    B.
    C. 21
    D.

27. *If Jenina is faster than Period, and Period is slower than Granite, and Granite is faster than Clifford, and Clifford can run a mile in 12.5 minutes, what is the minimum speed that Jenina could run a mile?*
    A.
    B.
    C. 3.14
    D.

28. *How should the following blocks be ordered?*
    A.
    B. C, D, A, B
    C.
    D.

29. *Which of the following does not fit:*
    Louisiana, Texas, Wyoming, Mexico, New Hampshire?
    A.
    B.
    C.
    D.

30. *What number should come next: 3, 9, 81, ___?*
    A.
    B.
    C.
    D. 516

31. If a group of eleven writers get together, and they all bring five books to exchange, but four of the titles have already been read, how many books will get exchanged?

    A. The Star of David portrays unity through the hexagram.

    B. It is a most miserable sight.

    C. a perfect number

    D. an odd number

32. If you re-arrange the letters C-S-A-M-O-S-H-T-I, what would you get?

    A.

    B. Cashmere

    C.

    D.

33. Stroke is to brain as _____ is to heart.

    A.

    B.

    C. love

    D.

34. Which of the following statements is true?

    A.

    B.

    C. This test is a sham.

    D.

35. Ivan was ranked 11th from the top and 11th from the bottom in his bowling tournament. If one player did not show up and was automatically disqualified, how many bowlers competed?

    A.

    B.

    C.

    D.

36. If the word "genius" means heart-broken, which of
    the following sentences is grammatically correct?
    A.
    B.
    C. I was born a genius.
    D.

37. Which of the following does not fit:
    butterfly, fractal, China, joystick?
    A.
    B.
    C. Fractal
    D.

38. Which of the following pieces would fit in this puzzle?

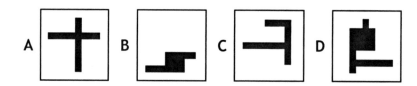

39. *Which of the following does not belong:*
    Washington, Fuji, Georgian, Pink Lady?
    A.
    B. Pink Lady
    C. Georgian
    D.

40. *When you re-arrange the letters C-E-I-L-I-B-M-E,*
    what IQ bracket would you fit into?
    A. Below average
    B. Average
    C. Above average
    D. Genius

There are 10 Commandments: I am your Lord and God, who brought you out of the land of Egypt... You shall have no other gods before me; You shall not take the name of the Lord your God in vain; Observe the Sabbath day, to keep it holy; Honor your father and your mother; You shall not murder; You shall not commit adultery;

You shall not steal; You shall not bear false witness against your neighbor; You shall not covet your neighbor's wife; You shall not desire your neighbor's house, his field, or his manservant or his maidservant, or his ox or his ass, or anything that is your neighbor's.

Kabbalists worship the 10 Sefirot.

chapter

10

: BUTTERFLY AFFECT

10

A discontented fractal causes a volcano to erupt in Sydney, Australia. The mystical reverberations in the opera house are destroyed.

A caterpillar spins a cocoon and emerges something new. A butterfly flaps its wings.

A man in England looks at the night, and in it, he sees what cannot be seen. His right eye squints against cold metal.

I'm afraid of caterpillars. I always have been. As a child, Me Thu cared for me, loved me, cherished me, and made me kill all the caterpillars that got into her house. She was terrified of them. I'm not her biological child, but she passed her phobia on to me.

I don't consider myself girlish, but I will yelp if I see a wiggling, squirming caterpillar anywhere near me.

In Prague, Adam stands in front of a mirror. His head is a smooth crystal ball, and he can tell no one's fortune with it. Sadly, he stares at himself. His face is gaunt and his body protrudes bones. He imagines that he's young and handsome. He imagines reaching into his mirror and releasing his own image. He doesn't know where it would go or how he would live without it, but he's sure that his hair will grow back when his reflection is gone.

In Costa Rica, a teenager does not find his destiny in a test. They have different standards for education in that country. At ten, children take tests that decide their future. It is nothing fail proof, something akin to a personality test, only in Costa Rica, you can fail.

In Texas, a small Asian man falls down. He doesn't grab his chest like people do in movies. He is outside. His fingers unwrap threads of grass, and a tint of green is embedded between the ridges of his palm. On the hot earth, he dreams of his daughter.

A Russian quadriplegic is beheaded in China.

In Mongolia, animals wail high-pitched tears. Unable to endure the torturous sound, the villagers hold a village meeting and decide that they must take action. Their children cannot sleep with such constant noise.

In his dream, his daughter is perfect. He cries because she is so perfect. She's a doctor, like he always wanted, and she's married with children. She has even moved back home with him and his wife so that he can play with his grandchildren all day long. In his dream, he is never tired. He remains strong and smiling.

As a child, I loved pecans. There was a pecan tree behind Me Thu's house. I collected them and stored them in an old shoebox. I stored and stored, as a squirrel would preparing for winter, but then I forgot about it. Children often forget things they love.

Weeks later, when I found the box, it overflowed with tiny caterpillars. Thousands of green beasts inched around, minute legs struggling against cramped space. I didn't cry though. Me Thu doesn't allow her children to cry. So I picked up the box and dropped it only once because of unsteady hands and catapulted it out the back door. I saw emerald rain onto dry, cracked dirt.

A man reads the newspaper.

His daughter coils toilet paper around her panties. He doesn't dream this. This is real. His daughter is embarrassed of herself, of her body. She can't tell him because she's worried he would be disappointed in her. She can't let him down. She knows that he has been let down by so many people that she couldn't be added to this list. She continues to wind the toilet paper. Looking down, she sees the stain imprinted on her jeans, bright red and unforgiving.

A woman pours a cup of coffee.

In a city much like Los Alamos, a physicist looks for the unseeable. He searches for dark matter by charting slight movements of large astronomical bodies. His eyes are weak from strain and he mistakes an asteroid for a planet.

My lover laughs at my fear of caterpillars. It's something he can't understand. There are many things he can't understand, and I can't explain them.

A caterpillar contorts its body closer to mine. I am terrified so I stomp on it. It isn't neon green like the ones in Texas. This one is large and black, a thick mound of fur stuck to my shoe. I laugh because they're Prada shoes and I just killed a bug with one of them. I find a strange comfort in killing. I don't even wipe my shoes before I walk back inside the apartment.

A woman travels to the eastern edge of Asia in search of dragons.

He dreams that his daughter is the genius that she was when she was a girl. He remembers the testing, the accolades. He couldn't understand English at the time, but he knew that she was special. He thinks she received a medal at a ceremony, but his memory is not so good. So he lies there on the grass and continues to dream.

A woman falls in love with her palm. With her fingers wrapped firmly around the handle of a coffee pot, she pours smooth black energy into a porcelain cup. She grips the plastic handle so tightly that her soft fingertips graze her palm. With the edge of her nail, she traces her life line. It is exactly as it should be. The man holding the cup nervously shuffles his newspaper.

A wife returns to find her husband sleeping on the grass. His body glistens sweat. She tries to lift him, but he's too big for her. She doesn't know what to do.

A boy loses a memory about a girl he once loved. Using the words he has left, he tries to rebuild her, but she is gone.

My memories are constantly shifting. I can hardly distinguish fact from fiction. Only today, I found a dead butterfly in my room. It was beautiful and lifeless. I wanted to preserve it, so I took a blade and carefully extracted its patterned eyes.

Looking at those eyes now, I find them disgusting, but still, I want them to remain with me. Carefully, I rip them through the center and again and again until there is nothing left of those eyes but the residue of life on my fingertips.

A couple buys a two-story house. The wife is obviously happy. She has a smirk glued to her face. She has worked her entire life to achieve this dream, and now, it is hers with only a little bit of debt dangling on a string in her peripheral vision. The husband glides his hand over her back, pausing at every crevice, worshipping her happiness.

They say that a butterfly flapping its wings in America can change the weather in Vietnam.